See You Next Sunday

ISBN 13: 978-1-59298-358-2

ISBN 10: 1-59298-358-8

Library of Congress Catalog Number: 2010936705

Book design and typesetting: Jill Blumer

Printed in the United States of America

First Printing: 2010

14   13   12   11   10   5   4   3   2   1

BEAVER'S POND PRESS

7104 Ohms Lane, Suite 101
Edina, Minnesota 55439 USA
(952) 829-8818
www.BeaversPondPress.com

To order, visit www.BeaversPondBooks.com or call 1-800-901-3480.
Reseller and special sales discounts available

See You Next Sunday

A NOVEL BY

MARY JOHNSON

BEAVER'S
POND
PRESS

Prologue

Usually while I wait in Soo Town for the train to rumble by, I use the time and the rearview mirror to check my nose and chin for the hairs I missed during my nightly tweezers pull. There was a time in my midfifties when I was absolutely sure I was well on my way to hirsutism. The stiff black hairs sprouting overnight above my lip and along my jaw were as coarse as the bristles on the back of my father's prize Duroc boar. Now that I'm on the backside of seventy, the unwelcome things are mostly white, but just as determined. My friends admit to the same problem and laughingly say it's yet another perk of the golden years, along with droopy breasts, belly fat, flabby upper arms, and a leaky bladder.

Today, though, nose hairs be damned, I found myself drawn to the colorful graffiti on the passing cars. There were the usual turf tags and political obscenities, with a definite proclivity toward the f-word, plus other blunt observations about the general state of the world, perhaps, I couldn't help thinking, more reflective of the nation's mood than any Gallup poll. And of course no artist of this ilk could possibly feel fulfilled without chalking a giant cannabis leaf and superimposing "pot" on it for the few folks who might not recognize the happy weed. The real eye-catcher for me, though, was the sixties platitude "Peace Sister" scrawled across an entire grain car. My own personal benediction, I thought, considering the Macy's shopping bag and its contents resting on the floorboard next to me.

Olson's Chapel had the urn ready for me. I signed the last check on Birdie's account, and John, my friendly mortician and occasional bridge partner, pushed the plain container across the desk and handed me a folded burgundy velvet drawstring pouch.

"You couldn't find a tractor, then?" I asked.

"It's the best we could do, Iv," he said. "Not much call for that kind of thing, I guess. Most people take the metal urn, or once in a while maybe a nice little wooden chest. Come to think of it, though," he paused, "I did find a loon for one lady . . . said her husband loved hearing them call across Pulaski. Kind of an eerie sound, to my way of thinking, but . . ." I didn't bother to tell John that Birdie wouldn't give a hoot for a fancy box, and why in God's name would he want to rest in a loon after he had finally, at long last, escaped the label that followed him for most of his seventy-nine years?

I felt like putting the bag on the seat and wrapping the seat belt around it. Birdie would want me to do that. He always buckled up. "I don't wanna get a ticket," he'd say, clapping his hands for emphasis. "Or go through the windshield . . . that's what happened to Bud Larson . . . found 'im in two pieces on the hood of his Buick . . . yep, right through the windshield!" Birdie would clap again and add, "But the guys down at Slat's said Bud lost his head a long time before that, when he started screwin' Tootie O." Then he'd cover his mouth and giggle, not because he understood the play on words or even the smut, but because Birdie loved the shock value of imagined blood and gore and the attention. His telling of that tale and others, no matter how often shared, was great entertainment to the beer drinking locals down at the bar. Birdie was always fair game for that kind of fun.

"Hey, Birdie," they'd encourage, winking at each other, "tell that story about Bud Larson."

* * *

The crossing arm swung up, and immediately the teenage punk in the jacked-up car perched on my back bumper laid on his horn and turned up his bass amps. If my grandson Jake were with me, he'd say, "Give him the bird, Grandma!" It was tempting, but a woman my age, with heart arrhythmia to boot, is wise to back away from any possible road rage, so I settled for a muttered "I could drag your butt with this old V8, kid." Jake would probably give me a high five for even that bland response.

I knew the driver from subbing at the middle school a few years back, Cody something-or-other. Dumb, but harmless, I thought. He was still on my tail at the Highway 55 stoplights, but by then, he'd recognized me and leaned out to holler, "Hey, Mrs. H., how's it hangin'?" As I said, not so smart.

"Not good, Cody," I wanted to say. "Not good."

* * *

When Olson's called that morning about the urn, my husband paused in his coffee refill to comment, "I thought we weren't going to have the memorial service until this summer when the kids could come."

I sighed. "Don't you listen to a word I say, Bill? I told you yesterday the mortuary doesn't store cremated remains."

"Oh, I guess I do remember your saying that." Then he laughed and added, "If you take a few of your nutcrackers down, you can put him on the fireplace mantel until June. What we should do, though, Iv, is take a little drive in the country and just let Birdie fly away." Bill flapped his arms and headed toward the den, conveniently oblivious to the puddle of coffee created by his simulated flight.

Grabbing a paper towel to blot up the spill, I snapped in sharp irritation, "I don't find that one bit amusing, Bill. I made a promise to Birdie that I'd take him home to be with Marion, and you know it!"

"I'm just kidding, Iv!" He shrugged and added, "Nothin' to get your undies in a bundle over . . ."

* * *

But now, as I headed north on Third, I reached over, picked up the Macy's bag, set it on the gray leather seat beside me, and voiced the question that had been stuck in my head since early Tuesday morning when the night nurse called.

"Oh, Birdie, how did we get to this place?"

Ivy May

My father had the well-intentioned but unfortunate notion he should name his children after old friends and departed relatives. He was determined, my mother told me later when I asked why we kids had such dumb names, that his sons would have names that meant something, stood out a bit from the rest of the herd, to use his words. Fortunately, fate intervened in the guise of several miscarriages, and there were only three of us—and one disappointingly, a daughter—to be stuck with odd handles.

I was chosen to immortalize the name of my grandfather's sister, who died of diphtheria back in Morristown, New York, in 1870, when she was barely five years old. Grandpa Henry often said it was a nice thing to remember the little tyke, taken down with his brother Charles and his parents so long ago. "My poor Ivy May," he'd say, shaking his head and blinking his eyes to squeeze out a reluctant tear or two, "called home long before her time." Then Grandpa would pull out his filthy snot rag, as Marion called it, the one he used for everything except blowing his nose. For that, he simply closed off one nostril with his forefinger and honked away, a totally disgusting habit, according to my mother. His faded back-pocket bandana was destined for more important chores, like wiping off the blade of his pocket knife after he'd quartered the seed potatoes—carefully leaving an eye in each piece—bobbed the tail of a newborn lamb, or helped my father castrate the spring barrows. And, to my mother's ire, it was also his table napkin. On wash day, she used a stick to toss it in with the porch rugs, which were thrown in at the very end after the whites, colors, and even the manure-spattered overalls were agitated in the old Maytag.

Grandpa Henry delighted in telling the sad tale of Ivy May's demise. It was embellished significantly over the years until, in the end, it was worthy of nothing less than a Sunday-night Hallmark Hall of Fame presentation. When I was very young, his creative history gave me horrible nightmares. What if I should wake up in the morning to find my own mother and father dead of some dread disease and be parceled off to spend my childhood with relatives who didn't love me? Once, in the early hours of the morning, I crept downstairs crying, and Mother took me into her warm bed, tucking my flannel night-gown around my cold feet and reassuring me that no such thing could ever happen. "Ivy May, honey," she soothed, "that was a long time ago. Remember, you've had the vacci-nation." Then she poked my father lying next to her and said in a hissed whisper, "I wish that fool father of yours would shut up about that business. It scares the wits out of Ivy May."

My father just snorted and rolled over on his back. "Yeah, old man . . . old story. God, Ruthie, you think I haven't heard it plenty of times myself? At least Uncle

John kicked the bucket before you had to hear him blow nonstop about doin' his Christian duty by Pa and Aunt Salome, takin' them in when nobody else wanted the poor little orphans. We never got through a family reunion without hearin' that crap. Sanctimonious old bullshitter!"

"Job! Watch your mouth!" My mother flung her arm across his chest. "Nobody did their Christian duty by Salome, and you know it! Her husband left her when she lost her hearing, and his folks, such wonderful servants of the Lord and all," my mother added sarcastically, "took her little girl away and weren't satisfied until they'd packed Salome off to St. Peter, where she stayed locked up until she died. Christian duty, Job? That's a laugh!"

"Shush. That's nothin' for Ivy May to hear."

"Well, you know it's true, Job. And nobody even cared enough to bring her back here when she died. There's a cheap headstone in the family plot, but she's not there." My father returned to his snoring without answering the accusation.

I curled under the covers, the worries starting anew. What if my mother got sent off to St. Peter to be locked up forever? That's what happened to my best friend's grandmother, too, when she wouldn't keep her clothes on. Dorie Ann told me about it during recess while we were waiting our turn to jump rope. Anything was better than watching smarty-pants LuAnn Miller do "salt and pepper" until she wet her pants or dropped down dead. I hoped for either result. "Yep," Dorie Ann said, "we looked out the kitchen window, and there was Grandma Stella in the garden, picking peas in her birthday suit. Pa said, "That's it! She can go crazy someplace else.'"

In the light of day, my worries eased as they always did, and I reasoned that this wasn't apt to happen because my mother wouldn't be caught dead in a sleeveless dress, much less her birthday suit.

* * *

When I took Shakespeare I from Effie Hunt back at Mankato State, I had to laugh at the bard's naïveté when he asked, "What's in a name?" Everything, I thought. And "A rose by any other name would smell as sweet"? Oh, come on! Who was he trying to kid? Granted, it was a sweet piece of iambic pentameter, but in my experience the substance ended there. Mostly, I thought, we lived up to our names—or worse, lived them down—for the rest of our lives. More than a few of us even have to get out of Dodge to escape the predestinations our names impose on us. That's what happened to me. As long as I stayed Ivy May, I was a worried, woebegone farm girl in a faded, flowered feed-sack dress, dark hair falling across downcast eyes, the perfect poster child for Appalachian Relief, and forever that Ames girl with the goofy brother. If I could add barefoot to my pathetic description, there could be no argument at all, but my mother didn't permit that summer joy. "Better to pinch your toes in tight shoes during the summer than get lockjaw from some rusty nail out in the barnyard," she warned. I worried about the possibility of that dire fate, too, and imagined my father prying my mouth open to dribble runny oatmeal down my throat.

My father was so right in thinking that our names would make us stand out from the herd. I was Ivy May in the midst of Karens, Mary Janes, Joys, and even more clever ones like Babs and Terry. But my two brothers fared even worse. Dad went way back to Great-grandfather Birdsel Ames to name my firstborn brother. How could any child not be odd with a name like Birdsel? I heard my mother say more than once that it was a god-awful shame, and she should have put her foot down. And Grandma Ada, who never found fault with her son, shook her head and said, "Oh, Job, I don't know about that name." But Birdsel it was, and then my father, clearly on a roll, came up with Marion for his second son. There was one of those somewhere in the Tann relations, a beekeeper, Grandpa Henry thought. I think I could have made do being a Marion; it's nowhere nearly as drippy as Ivy May. But I didn't blame my brother for wishing he were Tom or John instead of being named after a beekeeper who lived in Exeter, Rhode Island, two hundred and fifty years ago.

But as the saying goes, you play the hand you're dealt. And I guess we did.

Birdsel

Canning was my mother's summer labor and love. By the end of August, quart Mason jars filled with red tomatoes, pickles of every kind, green and yellow beans, corn, applesauce from the Whitney crab north of the house and the Wealthy orchard west of the garden, and succulent peaches and pears swimming in sweet syrup crowded the pine-plank cellar shelves. The most of it came from her huge and carefully tended garden. In the spring, when my father pitched the manure pile from the south side of the barn into the spreader, my mother was there to make sure the fragrant, aged stuff at the very bottom was the Miracle Grow that was tilled into her holy acre of paradise. She didn't much trust my father in her garden, and she watched Grandpa Henry like a hawk, rapping sharply on the pantry window when he tried to sneak a tiny carrot or two in late June.

Dad's chores were limited to ploughing the garden under in the fall, spreading and tilling in the spring fertilizer, and chopping up a few laths that had fallen from the snow fence so my mother could mark her rows and string a straight line of twine from end to garden end. It was then my mother's domain. Birdie, Marion, and I could enter only with permission, which was fine by us. Weeding and hoeing didn't appear to be a whole lot of fun anyway, if Mother's red face was any indication as she pulled the stubborn crabgrass, dusted the cabbage, and swatted mosquitoes.

Mother was proud to claim that her garden amply provided for the family table—from early spring lettuce, asparagus, and radishes to the large white russets unearthed in the fall, which we'd then store in the dark cellar bins. Unfortunately, though, peach and pear trees were scarce to nonexistent in southwestern Minnesota, and she had to depend on specials at Red Owl for good prices on lugs of these. In early August, when a lug of Alberta peaches sold for ninety-nine cents, my mother was willing to back the new Ford out of the garage and drive the nine miles to Worthington for this single purchase. After all, no housewife worth her salt would be without sauce. It was a meal staple, for both salad and dessert, for most of the year.

It was on such a day that Birdie, Marion, and I climbed into the back seat of the car for the ride into town. Mother would have preferred that we three stayed home with Dad, but he had other plans. "I'm fencin' in the far pasture," he said. "Don't know as I'll have time to watch the kids." At her sharp glance, he quickly added, "They'll be all over the place, scarin' the cows and runnin' down to the dredge ditch where I can't keep an eye on 'em." My father wasn't stupid. He knew that mere mention of the dreaded ditch and its foot of dirty water would be sufficient cause for my mother to worry about her brood's safety.

"Well, get in the car then. I don't have all day, you know. If the peaches are ripe, I might have to can yet this afternoon." Then she frowned at my father and said, "I thought you fixed the pasture fence last week."

"Thought so, too, Ruthie, but there's always one cow that's gotta keep stretching her noggin through the fence to get to the grass on the other side. Pretty soon there's a hole big enough for a calf to crawl through. Course, the little bugger's never smart enough to get back to its mama. It'll just stand there and blat its damn head off."

My mother tucked a strand of auburn hair into her braid and opened her purse to make sure she had a clean handkerchief. She was never one to tuck hers down the front of her dress like so many ladies did, especially those with the big bosoms. "You're not fixing John's part of the fence again, are you?" she asked. It was an unspoken law of the farm prairie that a good neighbor eyed his fence line every spring and fall and took responsibility for maintaining it from center to right until it met the corner post. It was a literal application of Robert Frost's well-known poetic line "Good fences make good neighbors" to be sure, but it served both fence and farmer well.

My father tipped his straw hat back and scratched his head before saying, "The thing is, Ruthie, I'm the one that's got the livestock that's gonna get out and bloat on John's alfalfa." Then he poked his head in the back car window to ruffle Birdie's blond head and say, "Mind your mother, you kids. Maybe she'll stop for an ice cream at Worthmore if you're good."

"Well, I could pick up some meat at the locker plant, I suppose." Mother's voice drifted off as she turned the key in the ignition and stepped on the gas, causing the engine to roar and my father to shake his head and wink at us. My mother never seemed to get the hang of driving the car, usually grinding the gears as she searched for second and third and then invariably lurching forward and killing the engine. My father also accused her of riding the brakes until the pads were shot. He backed away from the car and held up his hand in parting. "Give 'er hell, Ruthie!" He laughed and headed towards the tractor and two-wheel trailer . . . and a quiet afternoon of pasture fencing.

※ ※ ※

Red Owl was busy. No doubt other housewives were in search of cheap peaches and pears, too. We had strict orders not to touch anything if we expected an ice cream treat after the shopping was done. I suppose we looked like what we were, three farm kids checking out the candy counter, hoping that maybe we could persuade Mother to get us a pack of Black Jack. Marion prodded me, "Go ask Mom if we can get some Black Jack, Ivy May." She was back in produce, checking out the peaches. A frazzled young clerk was prying off corners of lugs so my mother could reach in to unwrap the tissue from a peach and see just how ripe the fruit was. I knew better than to ask until she gave me her attention. At five years old, I wasn't brave enough to interrupt her important task. Finally, she looked down and said, "What, Ivy May? What is it?"

"Can we get some Black Jack? Marion says we'll share."
I already knew then that just mentioning his name was a
good thing.

"Oh, all right," she sighed, and reached into her purse
for the nickel that would provide chewing satisfaction for
the next week. Marion would halve the sticks and divide
them between us. It never dawned on me to wonder what
happened to the extra piece. He plunked the blue-and-
black package in my hand and pushed me toward Marge
at the checkout counter. It should have been easy, but that
one pack of Black Jack bought on a summer's day changed
everything.

I didn't really know Marge, except that she was the
checkout lady at Red Owl. Mostly she seemed jolly to me,
and smart the way she worked the cash register with her
long fingers and their scarlet-painted nails, talking at the
same time. I put the Black Jack on the counter, pushed
the nickel beside it, and waited behind a woman with a
generous backside for my turn. "So, Marge," the woman
said, leaning across the counter and lowering her voice, "I
see Ruth Ames has her kids with today."

"Yah, Grace, good kids, you know. Too bad that oldest
one with the funny name . . . Birdie, I think it is . . . is so
slow. He's the little one, kind of a runt," she added, nodding
toward Marion and Birdie. "Always got a big grin on his
face, but . . ." Marge twirled her forefinger by her head and
gave the cash register an extra chink. "Must be special
hard for Ruth, her bein' a teacher and all before they got
married, then having a kid that can't learn for scratch."

Grace pursed her lips and nodded. "You know, Charlie did say he heard Job Ames had a boy that wasn't all there. A little moron, I guess." Then she added importantly, "Charlie's on the co-op board with Job, you know." The lady named Grace frowned and looked back at Birdie and Marion over by the candy counter. "It don't look like he's one of them mongoloids, though . . . I guess they call it some fancy name now . . . Down somethin'." The big butt finally moved forward, and Marge saw me for the first time. I thought she must be really hot because her face flushed as red as her dyed hair. My mother said once there was no way in God's creation she came on this Earth with that color hair.

"Oh, honey, I didn't see you standin' there. You just take that package of Black Jack and keep your nickel." She took my hand, pressed the nickel into my sweaty palm, and folded my fingers tightly over it. "You just keep that . . . a little something from Marge." By that time my mother had settled on three lugs of peaches and two of pears and was directing the produce boy to our car. Marge didn't waste any time ringing up the lugs.

"Come on. Get in the car and be quick about it if you want a cone," my mother ordered. She was all business with several hours of canning ahead. The peaches were dead ripe. We headed south on Humiston toward the other end of town, to the Worthmore Creamery and single-dip ice cream cones.

I counted my three half-sticks of Black Jack, tucked them in my dress pocket, and stood up to lean against the back of my mother's seat. "Mama," I asked, putting a hand on either side of her warm neck, "do we got a moron? That fat lady in the store said we did. And Marge said Birdie was slow. I wanted to tell her he could run faster than Marion even."

In the rearview mirror, I could see my mother's face crumble. The car surged forward, drawing me back onto the seat. "It's okay, Mama," I said. "We know Birdie can run fast. Don't cry."

"Oh, shut up, Ivy May!" Marion shouted, reaching across Birdie to punch my arm. "People say mean stuff about Birdie all the time. Just because you're a baby and don't know what's goin' on."

Birdie stuffed three half sticks of gum in his mouth and grinned. "Are we gonna git an ice cream cone?"

My mother wiped the tears with the back of her hand. "Let's get a double-dipper today. How about that, kids?" Then she added, her voice trembling, "And if know-it-all Marge with her fancy nails and dyed frizz thinks she'll ever see me in Red Owl again, she's got another thing coming!"

* * *

And double-dippers it was! We rolled the car windows down, which made for a breezy ride home and also called for efficient licking if we were to keep our ice cream from dripping on the upholstery. Mother was fussy about the car. "After all," she reminded us, "we were lucky to have our number drawn." Birdie, Marion, and I didn't know much about the war and getting our number drawn, but we were excited as all get-out when Dad let us ride to Windom with him to pick up the new '45 Ford. My mother wiped it inside and out every Saturday afternoon when the weather permitted. My father, though, didn't care so much; his first tractor, however, a '37 John Deere A, was a different matter entirely, its flywheel carefully oiled and checked for even the smallest specks of rust. But he wasn't above tossing a sack of chicken feed into the back seat of the Ford instead of using the trunk. That was sure to bring out the whisk broom and Mother's wrath. That day, with ice cream melting faster than we could lick, she kept her eyes on the road . . . and in the rearview mirror. Uncannily, she could do both. "Use your napkin, Birdie," she directed, "and don't lean over the front seat." And then, "Ivy May, sit down. For goodness' sake! It'll take a whole bottle of tetrachloride to get the spots off!" That magic solvent could only be purchased behind the counter from Mel at the local drugstore, but the powerful stuff could take a grease or sugar spot off from anything. Mother hid it on the top shelf in the pantry, and her admonishment that even a quick whiff of it would make us blind for life was enough to stifle our curiosity.

Marion escaped her scolding as usual, for not a drip of melted confectionary fell from his cone or even touched his finger. He knew exactly how to slick around the top of the sugar cone to shape the ice cream into a perfect peak. "Mom," he warned, "Birdie's makin' a big mess. His top dip's gonna fall off." The words were hardly out of

Marion's mouth before Birdie's double-dipper chocolate fell apart and landed on the floorboard to plop on alfalfa chaff and some cracked oats. "What'd I tell you?" Marion said, shaking his head and moving over closer to his window. Birdie grabbed the gooey mess on the floor and stuck it back on his cone, not bothered at all by the unappetizing topping.

* * *

My father was still out fencing when we returned, and that meant his afternoon coffee would have to be delivered to the pasture before any canning could be started. Mother was cross about the delay. She opened the trunk, reached in for a lug, and pushed through the yard gate. "Marion and Birdie, take a lug and set it on the kitchen table." Once in the kitchen, Mom set a match to the kerosene burner, pumped water into the pot, spooned in some Folgers, and set it on to boil, skipping her usual routine of stirring an egg into the dry grounds to make what she considered real coffee. Then she disappeared into the pantry to make a thick braunschweiger sandwich, which she wrapped in waxed paper and placed in the bottom of a lard pail. She added a piece of yesterday's spice cake and pressed the cover into place. "Ivy May, scoot down the cellar and get a Mason jar, one with the zinc lid screwed on tight so it's clean."

"Why can't Marion do it?" I asked, hating the dark basement with its steep stairs, dust and cob webs, and potato bins with long sprouts reaching for any light they could find. Marion told me more than once that they could grab me it if I got too close.

My mother didn't put up with whining. She pointed to the cellar door. "Ivy May Ames, now!" As I scurried down the steps, she muttered, "It wouldn't kill your father to go without his afternoon coffee, but I suppose it would be the end of the world as we know it if that ever happened." I took the first quart jar with a zinc lid that I saw and beat it back up to the kitchen. Mother filled the quart jar half full of hot coffee, screwed on the lid, and took two old potholders out of the bottom drawer. "You kids stay here. Marion, keep an eye on Birdie and Ivy May."

"Why do Birdie and me always get stuck with Ivy May?" Marion complained, pulling a kitchen chair close to the small desk in the corner by the pantry where my father kept his farm account books along side a Philco table radio and a few back issues of the *Farm Journal*, *Wallace Farmer*, and the *Sioux City Journal*. Marion never missed *Sky King* on WNAX Yankton, the only station that came in without lots of static in our neck of the woods.

"Because I said so, Marion." And my mother quickly reached across him and clicked the radio off. "There," she said in a voice that all of us knew meant business, "now maybe you'll understand that I mean it when I ask you to do something." She grabbed the lard pail, grasped the Mason jar of coffee with the potholders, and headed for the entryway. "And Marion, it wouldn't hurt you a bit to practice your piano lesson while I'm gone. Otherwise, it's a dollar wasted and a trip to Worthington for nothing, and we don't have time or money for such foolishness." The back screen door slammed, and she was gone.

Marion couldn't resist a parting shot, "Why don't you ever tell Ivy May to practice? She's still just playin' with one finger." He immediately turned the radio back on. "Get lost, Ivy May! Go play with your dolls or get Birdie to pull you in the wagon." As Birdie and I pushed open the door, he added, "And don't tell Mom I didn't practice or you're in for it."

We found the wagon under the grape arbor, and I climbed in, folding the tongue back so I could steer. Off we went, across the gravel driveway and down the path by the alfalfa field until we reached the cow lane, Birdie pushing as hard as he could and making put-put noises as if he were driving the A instead of moving a rusty red wagon along. Finally he stopped, red-faced and out of breath. "Get out, Ivy May, or I'll dump you in a cow pie." I scrambled out, the back of my dress clinging to my behind, wet from the rainwater that had collected overnight in the wagon. Birdie laughed and then danced around me. "Ivy May peed her pants. Ivy May peed her pants!" I slipped under the barbed-wire fence and raced down the lane to the pasture and my mother's arms, wailing as if the world were coming to an end and affirming Marion's frequent accusation that I was just a big bawl baby. Actually, what he usually teased was "Bawl baby ripsy, sucka Mama's titsy," always conveniently out of earshot of my mother.

My mother and father were sitting close, shielded from the hot afternoon sun by the big rear tractor tire. His arm looped across her slumped shoulders, and his face seemed red even under the dark tan. And then, almost lost in my mother's sobs, I heard the "moron" word for the second time that day. Even a five-year-old can sense something deeper than her own tears. I stopped my caterwauling and settled down to comfort my mother, but she would have none of it. "I thought I told you to stay home," she said sharply as she spotted Birdie at the end of the lane. "Can't a person get a moment's rest from you kids?"

My father sighed and said, "Best finish the fencing and get home for chores. Suppose you got peaches to can, Ruthie. Supper gonna be late?"

By this time Birdie had climbed up on the seat of the A. My mother sounded her immediate alarm. "Birdsel, get down from there right this minute! You've got no business on the tractor at all." She looked to my father for support, but instead he cranked the flywheel; once the iron beast started to pop, he settled on the seat behind Birdie.

"Let's go, Bird." He covered Birdie's hand with his own and slowly, but steadily, pushed in the clutch. "See, if you do it that way, you won't jerk the hell out of the hitch."

My mother was beside herself. "Job!" she shouted after the tractor. "He can't do that. He'll get hurt and then what?" Either my father didn't hear her or he didn't care. They headed across the pasture, Birdie sitting tall and proud as he steered the A.

Marion

Marion was both blessed and cursed. He was, without any doubt, my mother's golden child, able to learn quickly, especially good with numbers. And as if that were not enough, a benevolent God also graced Marion with blond hair, dazzling blue eyes, and a strong chin to complement his considerable athletic, musical, and artistic talent.

Even in second grade, Marion filled sketchbook after sketchbook with beautiful horses, their manes and tails flowing as they galloped over green pastures. They were his fantasy steeds, in no way even remotely related to our own old, swaybacked pony, who, my father complained, was good-for-nothing crow bait that should be shipped off to the glue factory before we wasted any more alfalfa on her. I was almost glad when Dixie died from eating some bad silage. In my naïveté, I thought that if she escaped the glue factory, then there had to be a place for animals, too, like the "eternal resting place" Grandpa Henry was always talking about. Dixie would be "gathered up by the Lord," as Grandpa put it.

I visualized her being enraptured, albeit from the cow yard, up and away to a place of glory, but it didn't seem very likely when the rendering truck came. The hauler wrapped a log chain around Dixie's hind legs and cranked her up into the truck, her bloated body banging against the end gate as it was pulled up and over to land with a soft thud on other dead animals in the truck. Then he handed Marion a box of chocolate-covered cherries, which my brother put to his nose and then promptly threw into the five-gallon pail along side the garage that my father used for grease rags. "I hope he doesn't expect us to eat this crap," he said, knowing full well he had used a sinful word that would have its own retribution if our mother heard it, the boldest words in her vocabulary being such expressive jewels as "Egad!" and "My word!" Marion pinched his nose in disgust before adding, "They're probably full of maggots, too."

"Fussy little shit," the driver muttered, climbing into the truck cab. And whatever it was that leaked from the end gate as he bumped down the rutted driveway didn't smell at all like the paradise Grandpa described. That evening, after my father had finished reading the *Daily Globe*, he frowned at us kids and asked about the chocolate-covered cherries at the bottom of the grease rag pail. Marion just shrugged and kicked me under the table. I knew that meant "Keep your mouth shut, Ivy May." It was left to Birdie to tell the truth. "Marion said there was maggots in 'em." My father laughed and said he wouldn't be a bit surprised. Marion didn't sketch any horses for a long time after that. I guess he thought it would be disloyal to Dixie.

Arithmetic was so simple for Marion that he didn't even have to make flash cards for multiplication and division, and he passed the timed tests on each set the first time around. But as much as I envied his drawing and adeptness at numbers, I was downright jealous of Marion's gift of music. My father had picked up an old upright at a farm auction. In its prime, it had been a player piano, but that function was long gone. As far as key action and sound, though, it was plenty good enough for his chording and my first piano lessons. I was smugly happy. For once, I would be able to do something Marion couldn't.

When my mother suggested that maybe he should take lessons, too, I was crushed—spitefully angry would be a more accurate description. Marion took to the piano like a Beethoven prodigy. At the end of three months, I was still playing out of book one of the Thompson Series and barely that, pretty much one finger at a time. And Marion, well, Marion was playing chords and even crossing hands when he played "Tea for Two" out of book three. It was galling. Then, when Mrs. Larson, our piano teacher, asked him to play it during the free-will offertory at the spring concert of the Worthington Male Chorus, I was literally ill. She told my mother that people would be so impressed . . . a good-looking young boy playing a difficult piece so beautifully.

And Marion did a masterful job, keeping his wrists up and level and elbows in, adding expression as though he really "felt" the music he was playing. My mother was misty-eyed with pride. Privately, Marion told me it was kind of a stupid song and that the kids in school would call him a "fruit" if they ever heard him play that silly thing. Later, when Mrs. Larson introduced him to ragtime,

Marion fell in love with the difficult tempos and rhythms. Scott Joplin's "Maple Leaf Rag" was the last piece I heard him play, and then the piano was silent except for Grandma Ada's yearly old-time chording rendition of "Over the River and Through the Woods" on Thanksgiving Day.

Town School

As it turned out, Marion knew what he was talking about that fateful day when he said I was too little to know what was going on with Birdie. When Shady Nook closed in the spring of '44 and we were bused into town school that fall, I was quickly baptized into the fire of school bullying. We were second on for the morning ride, and my mother had us out waiting for the bus that first day, long before it was due. She was nervous, retying the sash on my feed-sack dress over and over to get the bow just right. "You three sit in the front seat," she said, "and, Marion, when you get to school, don't you run off and leave Ivy May and Birdie stranded."

Marion frowned, "I'll get Birdie to his room, but Ivy May can find her own. She's in second grade, isn't she? And why do we have to sit up front? That's for the little sissies . . ."

"Marion," my mother warned, "do as I say."

"It's always me," he grumbled. "Well, is Birdie supposed to go to the fifth- and sixth-grade room or what? Miss Koster didn't give him a pass on his report card, did she?" My mother put her finger to her lips in a quick shush and bent down, moistening a corner of her apron to dab at the jelly stain on the front of Birdie's striped overalls. Then she straightened his cap, enfolded his thin body in her arms, and held him close to whisper vehemently, "You just walk right into that room and take your seat like the rest of the kids."

"Yeah, sure," Marion muttered sarcastically, "that'll really show 'em." Then he added, "What if the teacher makes him leave, then what?"

"Birdie has just as much right to be there as anybody else."

"Here it comes!" Marion shouted as the bus came down the hill from the Bensons'. He grabbed Birdie's hand. The bus ground to a stop on the rough gravel road, and the door swung open.

"Watch out, kids," Mr. Anderson advised. "It's a big step."

"All right if they sit in the front seat, Howard?" my mother asked.

"Looks like it's empty, Ruthie," he joked.

The Benson girls—Miriam, Helen, and Lucille—were in the back of the bus, sharing a seat. Helen had been an eighth grader with us at Shady Nook the previous year, but the other two were already in high school. We didn't really neighbor with them, but their father was in the threshing ring, and when it was our turn, my mother hired Miriam to come over and help with the cooking and keep an eye on us kids. Usually Helen and Lucille came, too. My mother didn't like it much. In her estimation, it was two extra mouths to feed. She figured Inez Benson sent them along because then she didn't have to make a meal that day. She'd drop the three girls off a little after eight on her way to Worthington to spend the day with her mother and shop for school bargains at JC Penney.

John Benson was a curious sort to us kids. He was deeply tanned all over, or so it seemed to us, mainly because he wore bib overalls and nothing else, no shirt or underwear as far as we could see, which was pretty far down due to his unbuttoned side vents. "He could at least have the decency to button up his pants," my mother grumbled.

Dad just laughed. "You been peekin' again, Ruthie?"

"That's disgusting, Job!"

John Benson liked his tomatoes sliced into a big cereal bowl and liberally covered with cream and a heaping spoonful of sugar. After the meal, he always put his chair back up to the dining-room table and stopped in the kitchen. "Thank you kindly for the good meal, Ruthie. Them were some awful good tomatoes."

* * *

Despite all that, it was comforting to see familiar faces that first day of town school. "Hey, you kids, come back here and sit with us if you want to," invited Lucille. "C'mon," she beckoned with her hand.

Marion was barely out of the front seat before Mr. Anderson caught his eye in the rearview mirror and said, "What'd your mother tell you, sonny? You'd best sit right there with your little brother and sister." Marion's ears turned red, but he sat down, staring straight ahead. Birdie didn't care where we sat; he was far away in his own world, making putt-putt sounds and pretending his lunch pail was a steering wheel. I had the window seat, but even gazing out the window at the late August cornfields didn't stop the growing nausea. My head was swimming and my stomach rolling by the time we were halfway through the route.

Nobody paid much attention to us until we stopped at Charley Meyers's farm. The Meyers had eleven kids, and people liked to gossip about the goings-on at their place. One story even had it that one of the girls put her hand on a stump and dared her older brother to chop it off with the ax . . . which he did. My mother said it was rubbish, and if it did actually happen, decent folks shouldn't be talking about it. But when the Meyers girls followed their big brothers onto the bus, I couldn't help looking to see if any hands were missing. The hands were all there, but one seemed a little short on fingers. Marion leaned across Birdie and glared, "Stop staring, Ivy May! You wanna get whacked?"

The Meyers all headed for the back. It didn't take me long to figure out that was where the action was. Mr. Anderson couldn't quite manage to keep an eye on the back-seat activities and maneuver the bus around the potholes in the gravel road at the same time. He tried, but he wasn't a fair match for the Meyers crew, especially Willy, who immediately told the Benson girls to move their fat asses out of his seat. Helen and Miriam were quick to crowd into another, but Lucille wouldn't budge. "That's bullshit, Willy," she declared. "You don't own the back seat," and she braced her knees against the seat in front of her.

"Wanna bet?" Willy grabbed for her but lost his balance when Mr. Anderson slammed the bus to a stop and yelled for him to take a seat up in front. I was tasting bile by this time, and I knew my morning pancakes were going to end up on the floor if I didn't touch ground soon.

Thankfully, Willy sat down. I guess he knew Mr. Anderson would kick him off if he didn't behave, and it would be a long walk to school. He wouldn't dare go home because Old Man Meyers had a reputation for being abusive in his discipline. Charley often bragged, "If any one of those little sons o' bitches gets a whippin' in school, there'll be another one waitin' at home!"

Willy sat across from us, his long legs stretched across the aisle. He stared at the three of us for a while and then said with obvious derision, "What's that little turd doing with his lunch pail?" When there was no answer, he grabbed Birdie's cap and held it high over his head. "Hey, dummy. I'm talkin' to you."

Marion flew out of his seat like an irate Banty rooster. "Give that back, you big jerk!" he shouted. Willy sailed Birdie's cap toward the back of the bus, and I vomited my breakfast on everything within projectile distance— my feed-sack dress, Birdie's new oxfords, the floor, and the steps. I somehow even managed to spatter the door windows. Willy Johnson gagged, stood up, and hollered for the entire bus to hear, "Oh, my God, the little shit just puked her brains out!"

Howard told Birdie and me to stay on the bus until all the kids got off and then he'd help us. I sat there, tears running through the spittle, wishing I was back at Shady Nook as the kids held their noses and tried to jump over the sour, curdled mess. Marion was the first one off, grabbing the handrail and swinging down with the grace of a natural athlete . . . and the haste of a brother who couldn't escape his brother and sister quickly enough.

Grandma Ada lived right next to the school, so Howard took us over there after he wiped us off as best he could with an old towel he used for cleaning the bus windows. Grandma shook her head and took us into the kitchen, where she did a better job on Birdie's new shoes and carefully pulled my dress over my head to get it soaking in a pan of soapy water. "Don't want the stains to set. Be as good as new, Ivy May," she said and went to the far wall to ring the operator. I heard her tell Alvera to give my mother a jingle and tell her I threw up on the bus and needed a fresh dress. "Probably send along some clean panties, too," she added, lowering her voice. Everybody rubbered on our line, so within minutes the whole county probably knew that Ivy May Ames puked on the bus on her first day of town school, dirtied her dress, and even soaked her underwear through.

* * *

Grandma Ida gave Birdie a filled raisin cookie and a tin pie plate and told him to sit on the back porch and play tractor while she cleaned me up. My father had gone to Worthington to get a new plowshare, but luckily our neighbor to the south, Emil Froeling, had stopped in for morning coffee and a little gossip, and he was more than willing to deliver a fresh dress and clean panties to a damsel in distress. He took one look at me, shivering half naked in my undies, and laughed. "Ain't the end of the world, Ivy May. I'll be damned if we ain't all lost our lunch some time or 'nother." Grandma Ada shook her head at him in disapproval, but Emil didn't say "Pardon my French" or anything like that.

My second-grade class was already through with reading and doing double-digit addition by the time Grandma knocked on Miss Smith's door and gently pushed me inside. The kids all turned in their seats, and I knew from their stares and snide smiles that even the town kids had heard about the country hick, Ivy May Ames. Miss Smith was quick with her reprimand. "Students, just turn around and get busy. This does not concern you." Then she took my hand and led me to an empty desk at the back of the first row, right by the door. "We're reviewing our addition facts," she said, pointing to the problems on the board and opening a tablet for me. I had no idea what to do. At Shady Nook, I mostly colored and looked at picture books from the little library, whose collection only amounted to a hundred or so books stacked on a couple of planks along the cloakroom wall.

I thought seriously about throwing up again, but then there was a knock on our classroom door and Miss Smith left the first graders to answer it. An older lady poked her head in the door and beckoned to my teacher. She looked cross. "Can I talk to you for a minute, Louise?"

When Miss Smith stepped out, she left the door ajar, just enough to keep an eye on us while she talked. It was then I saw Birdie. He grinned and waved. "The Ames boy can't be in my room," the lady whispered Miss Smith. "What am I supposed to do with him?" She pursed her lips, frowned, and added, "He's obviously very slow. I don't go along with those parents who think they can send their retarded children to regular school. It's not fair to the other students." She sounded mad at Birdie because she thought he was slow.

"But Birdie's not slow," I blurted out. "He's fast as can be. You should see him race Marion, and Marion could run faster than any of the kids at Shady Nook, even the eighth graders."

Miss Smith turned quickly and put her finger to her lips "Ivy May, please." There was more talking outside the door . . . about my mother being a teacher and how she should know better. The crabby teacher said my mother was touchy about Birdie, whatever that meant. Then the best thing in the world happened. Miss Smith led Birdie into the classroom, moved a desk right next to mine for him, and brought an empty paste jar full of broken crayons and a huge stack of pictures for him to color. Every once in a while, she stopped by Birdie's desk, smiled, and said, "Try to stay in the lines, Birdsel, and don't use quite so much green." Birdie's favorite color was green, just like our John Deere.

* * *

Birdie, Marion, and I were first off the bus after school. I was in a hurry to get up the lane and tell my mother about Willy Meyers. Marion must have sensed my urgency because he grabbed my arm and pinched hard. "Don't tattle to Mom about what happened on the bus, Ivy May, or I'll sneak in your bedroom tonight and hold the pillow over your head until you go nuts like you always do."

I pulled away, rubbing the red marks from Marion's pinch. "But Willy Meyers was mean to us. He was making fun of Birdie."

"Yeah and so what? Your tattlin' won't change anything, and it just makes Mom sad. Remember last summer at Red Owl?" I did.

"Marion," I asked. "do you think Birdie's a runt? That's what Marge said."

Marion just looked at me. "You're weird, Ivy May. Bet I can run and touch the yard gate before you can." And he was off, leaving me trailing behind. He was waiting for me at the gate. "Remember what I said. Keep your mouth shut."

Runts

"April is the cruelest month, breeding lilacs out of the dead land," according to T.S. Eliot, anyway. My father's assessment of early spring was less poetic and a bit more pithy. "It's a bitch," he'd exclaim, for fragrant lilacs were still weeks away on the windy plains of southwestern Minnesota, usually not blossoming until the middle of May and lasting for Memorial Day bouquets to bedeck the school gymnasium for the community remembrance of the departed, military and otherwise.

Spring on the farm meant muddy ruts in the lane, so deep and treacherous that the Ford had difficulty navigating them, even in first gear. We'd have to make a run for it, and those attempts usually churned to a halt, leaving my father cursing and the car bogged down up to the running boards a good hundred yards from the county gravel road. Without knee boots we were doomed, taking to the water-filled ditches on either side as an acceptable alternative to the suction of the saturated clay, which could cause even a careful person to walk right out of his boots.

But the worst of spring was the manure, knee deep in the cattle loafing shed, steaming mountains of it outside every cattle and hog barn door and even a nostril-clearing, noteworthy heap alongside the chicken house.

Our neighbor to the south, stopping in for a morning cup of coffee, aptly described the situation as he tapped a little tobacco from his Sir Walter Raleigh tin onto the thin paper and carefully rolled his own cigarette. "It's time to pitch shit, Job!" Timing was everything. If my father was to spread the winter's poop collection on the fields, it had to be accomplished before the frost was out of the ground; otherwise, the ground would be too soft and the tractor and spreader would get mired in clay up to the axles. Even then, the low spots and peat ground would have to be avoided. So when it was deemed all-systems-go, my father hauled manure from sunrise to sundown, leaving the dooryard and driveway strewn with stinky clods that fell from the spreader. The stench permeated everything, including Monday's wash hung on the orchard clothesline. The bed sheets didn't smell like apple blossoms and spring rain, but something more akin to barnyard Brut.

Spring was rarely a time of marital harmony in the Ames household. My mother was beside herself. Desperate in her attempts to keep up with the filthy overalls and chore coats, she had the Maytag moved to the back porch so the smell and mess wouldn't be in the kitchen. She lined the entryway with fresh newspapers daily to protect the linoleum from mud-caked and manure-spattered boots, and, of course, the plastic shipping cover went back on the davenport to remain until corn picking was over in the fall.

Spring was calving and farrowing. Those not involved in the process might be able celebrate the simple joy of

new life, but to my father, every cow that dropped a still-
born and every sow who lay on her litter or cannibalized
a few of her own piglets was a cause for sharp economic
concern. Dead animals did not put feed in the trough or
food on the table.

My father loved his pigs, never tiring of their snuffling or the clanging waterers, which broke the night
silence of the farmyard. All visitors to the farm were
obliged to take the short walk to pig house and admire
his red Durocs or lean Chester Whites. When the sows
farrowed in late March and early April, he insisted that
my mother, Birdie, Marion, and I check out each new
litter. One Saturday morning, when I was racing around
with Shep, our old, multicolored sheepdog, my father
beckoned me into the pig barn. I looked over the board
fence of the pen, my eyes adjusting to the semidarkness,
and watched a big litter of newborn piglets nurse their
mother. Each one was tightly attached to a teat, sucking
vigorously while the sow grunted in satisfaction . . .
except for a little wobbly one that could find no place at
the table. My father watched for a while, frowning, then
reached over the partition to grab the piglet by the hind
legs, lifting it up and over. Before it could even let loose
a weak squeal, he reached for the claw hammer resting
on a nearby nail and sharply struck the tiny thing on the
head before tossing it out the door, where it landed life-
less on the manure pile.

"Stop your blubbering," he said, seeing my tears. "It
would've died anyway." I could hear the exasperation in

his voice. My father didn't like crying, often telling us if we didn't stop, he'd give us something to really cry about. But then, softening his voice, he put his arm around my shoulder. "It's a runt, Ivy May, and it'd never amount to enough to pay for the feed. I just put the poor little fella out of his misery."

"But I would have taken care of it," I sobbed. (Had I known about Charlotte's Wilbur, I could have refuted his assertion, but that feel-good farm tale was almost a decade away from its telling.) Anyway, by that time my father was already on his way to the cow yard and an overdue Hereford heifer laboring in the mud to deliver her first calf.

"Damn," I heard him mutter. "The trouble never ends."

I wanted to climb the manure pile, take the runt, and bury it somewhere in an old shoe box lined with some leftover velvet from my mother's sewing box. But instead I thought back to that summer day when Marge at Red Owl called Birdie a little runt, and I knew right then that Marion and I had to find a way to help Birdie amount to something. Otherwise he could end up in the manure pile.

"Ivy May," my father shouted from the cow yard. "Git to the house! Tell you mother I need her. I'm gonna have to pull this calf or we'll lose the heifer, too!"

Hallowed Ground

The haymow of the farm's old hip-roofed barn was the hallowed playground of our childhood. It was our very own Lake Okoboji Amusement Park. Of course, there was no rickety roller coaster or giant tumbling barrel to attempt to navigate without ending up with skinned knees and elbows, but instead an unmatched and mystical place of pungent alfalfa darkness, the promise of secret tunnels and unexpected delights like a newly born litter of barn kittens or a friendly stray dog that had found warm refuge for the night after being tossed out to fend for itself by some careless town folk. There were mountains of bales and always some loose piles of timothy from the lowland. In late August, when the last cutting was safely stored away, Birdie, Marion, and I would climb to the very top stack and jump, sailing into the sea of hay below.

Along the length of roof was the trolley that carried the slings of bales or loose hay to the back of the mow or wherever there was room for more. Marion discovered that if we pulled the trolley all the way to back of the barn, the three of us could make a run for it, catch the fist-sized rope, and swing almost to the other end, the well-oiled trolley moving us along at what we considered to be lightning speed. That was one thing about Marion; he was really good at figuring out how to do fun stuff.

High up in the far north corner of the haymow was the rope room, a tiny cranny, just big enough to crawl into, but a perfect hideout nonetheless. Birdie, Marion, and I scampered up the wall ladder and into the niche many a time to get away from the bad guys of our imaginary games. The rope room held the coils of ropes that operated the trolley and the long rope that was hitched to the team or the John Deere to lift the slings out of the hay rack and up into the haymow. After that day in the pasture, Birdie took over the task of driving the tractor for this part of the haying, and with it he seemed to leave our childhood games behind. He basked in my father's praise, and I think he decided that it was foolish to keep on coloring pictures when something as important as driving a tractor was within his power.

My mother was never comfortable with Dad's decision. The first time Birdie handled the tractor without my father's guiding hand, she was out of house and into the dooryard without even stopping to shake the flour from her morning's bread-making off her hands. "Job!" she screamed. "Get Birdie off that tractor this minute. What in the world are you thinking? He can't do that!"

My father put up his hand. "He's doin' just fine, Ruthie. He's doin' just fine. Get back to your kneadin'." My mother reluctantly returned to her potato bread, but during haying she spent most of her time looking out the kitchen window, as if her close watch could keep Birdie and the rest of us safe.

There was one other delight in the haymow, a forbidden one. It was the giant grain bin in the northeast corner in which my father used to store his oats or barley crop. The bin's chute opened downstairs behind the horse stalls. The three of us discovered the bin a long time before my father found out. We would climb the outside ladder and jump into the bin, sometimes feet first, other times free-falling on our stomachs, either way nearly burying ourselves up to our necks in the oats or barley. Unless he was looking for help with the chores, my father didn't pay much attention to what we kids were doing, so when we heard him below one afternoon taking the harnesses off the wall, there was no great worry on our part.

Dad didn't get angry very often, but when he did, he put the fear of God in us. All three of us were in the bin, thrashing to get out of the shifting grain, when he peered over the edge and hollered, "What the hell do you kids think you're doin'?

"We were just havin' a little fun . . ." was Marion's weak reply.

"You get your butts out of there right now and stay out!" My father waited while we climbed up the inside ladder. He was red in the face and breathing hard as he grabbed us one by one by the seats of our pants to haul us over the wall of the bin and toss us into the hay below. We knew we were in for a good scolding, or worse, when he hopped off the bottom rung and turned to face us. "Whose dumb idea was it to jump in the oats?"

"Birdie wanted to . . ." ventured Marion.

My father grabbed Marion by the collar and shook him. "Don't go blamin' Birdie. I know he didn't come up with a crazy stunt like that." He pulled off his cap and wiped his forehead with the back of his hand before continuing. "God Almighty, that grain can suck you right down, and by the time somebody digs you out, you won't be breathin'. You'll have a snoot full of oats and no air. You got that, you little buggers? If I ever catch you doin' it again, you won't be able to sit for a week." Then he shook his head. "Your mother'd have apoplexy if she ever found out." That was a serious understatement. In fact, "apoplexy" was probably a weak word to describe the outburst that was sure to be leveled first at my father and then us kids. Mom would be livid at first and then follow that with her cold-shoulder treatment for at least the next couple of weeks.

My mother was one of those worried, fatalistic souls who almost always painted the worst scenario in any situation. When we went swimming, she warned us not to dive because she knew a boy who tragically broke his neck when he foolishly jumped into shallow water. When our 4-H club had a tobogganing party, she recalled an unfortunate youth who ended up with a broken back. When we tried to ride old Dixie, she reminded us of the neighbor boy who was dragged for miles by his spooked pony. And youth fellowship hayrides were totally out of the question after Grandma Ada told her about some poor little girl who ended up nothing but a vegetable after tumbling off the wagon and hitting her head on a big rock.

I tried to come up with a mental image of a little girl turned vegetable, but I couldn't grasp the idea of her morphing into a carrot, beet, or potato. I figured Marion would know, so I asked him. He rolled his eyes and said it was kind of like being a moron, only worse. "You know," he added, "like Poopsie down the street from Grandma Ada's. He just lays there in his diapers even if he is a grown-up." Marion poked a finger at my head. "Nothin' upstairs, Ivy May."

"Birdie's got somethin' upstairs, doesn't he, Marion? And he's not a runt, is he?" I asked, remembering the piglet tossed out on the manure pile.

Marion stared at me and then pushed me on my back side, hard. "Ivy May, you make me sick! You're always blabbin' about stuff that makes Mom feel bad. Can't you keep nothin' to yourself? Who needs your two cents, anyway?"

I guess it's no wonder I turned out to be a worrywart. I came by it naturally, a gift from my mother's Scandinavian heritage and the belief that we are at the mercy of nature and a mostly vengeful god. My father was a different sort entirely. Unlike my mother, he embraced life. He accepted it as it was, joy and sorrow, trusting in the ultimate fairness of it and his own strength to deal with whatever wasn't. His favorite poem, besides "The Village Smithy" and "The Cremation of Sam McGee," was W. E. Henley's "Invictus," especially the ending line, "I am the master of my fate. I am the captain of my soul." Dad could recite it from memory, his deep voice ringing out with power and conviction.

My father's warning about the dangers of jumping in the oat bin pretty much fell on deaf ears. It was simply too much fun to give it up. Birdie, Marion, and I were just more careful. One of us, usually Birdie, was the lookout. When he saw my father leave the pig house and head toward the barn, he hollered, and we scrambled out of the bin and into a nearby bale fort for safe cover. Like Marion said, "What Mom and Dad don't know, won't hurt 'em." I'm pretty sure he heard that from Grandpa Henry, who let us tie our coaster wagon to the back of the corn planter for a free ride while he clucked to the horses to move along and not hang back on the double-tree.

My Dog Has Fleas

Grandma Ada came from a long line of musical folk, self-taught for the most part, with only a few lessons here and there and those mostly from relatives. Her grandfather was a bugler in the Civil War with Company C of the Second Ohio Cavalry until he was mustered out at Columbus, Ohio, with a heart disability in 1862. Birdie, Marion, and I always wondered what happened to the bugle, but mostly debated if he'd carried one of those big sabers and killed somebody. No one seemed to know. The Ames clan was different story.

They were into beekeeping, not fiddling. Grandpa Henry admitted without embarrassment he couldn't carry a tune in a bushel basket, but his tin ear and droning monotone didn't prevent him from raising his voice to the Lord on a Sunday morning or persuading Grandma Ada on Thanksgiving Day to pull out the piano stool after dinner was over and dishes done and chord a rollicking "Turkey in the Straw." Grandma's piano was a huge, scarred old upright that dominated the north wall of her small, drafty parlor. The ivories were cracked and yellowed, and almost any key, black or white, was determined to stick just when she needed it most. Dad said Grandma Ada went without teeth for a whole year because she used her egg money to buy the piano instead of dentures.

Of course, Grandma Ada's chording always brought out my father's fiddle and harmonica, and in the afternoon, our stomachs groaning under the load of second helpings of turkey, sage dressing, and smooth, rich gravy, was celebrated with Civil War songs—"The Vacant Chair" and "Johnny Comes Marching Home" being everyone's favorites—and always "The Irish Washerwoman," numerous requests from the green *Tabernacle Hymnal*, and ditties like "The Picnic Song."

It was also show-off time for the cousins. One by one, we displayed our talents, or lack of them. I fumbled my way through an easy version of "Minuet in G," hitting my usual number of sour notes, and Cousin Amelia sang all four verses of "What a Friend We Have in Jesus," closing her eyes and lifting her hands to the heavens to implore God's grace and praise his holy name. Birdie covered his mouth and started to giggle until my mother reached over and grabbed his ear.

Then it was Marion's turn, and my pitiful grasp of music, along with my self-esteem, took a hit that dropped me down past my baggy socks. Marion soundly struck the opening notes of Nemerowsky's "Alla Mazurka" and then flew through the complicated runs with perfect fingering and nary a stumble. It was dead quiet until he hit the last note, a single low G in fortissimo, leaving the relatives shaking their heads in awe and bursting into bravos and calls for an encore. Marion obliged with "Maple Leaf Rag" and stole the afternoon a second time. I went and sat on the upstairs steps with Birdie, where he'd fled to save his ear from further twisting.

After the talent show, Grandma Ada was back at the piano. "How about 'Roll Out the Barrel?' That's a good one to get your feet tappin'. Job, you play the spoons." My father grabbed a chair and two tarnished, silver-plated spoons off the table, positioning them on his upper leg just above the knee, did a practice clatter, and away they went. Birdie peered through the banister spools to watch my father's deft hands as they moved in rhythm to the polka.

"Think I could do that, Ivy May?" he asked, slapping his hands against his legs. "Bet I could." Then he left me on the stairs and moved to stand by my father's shoulder.

Dad looked up at him. "Wanna try it, Birdie?" he asked, handing the spoons over and motioning to his empty chair as he stood up and took a harmonica out of a breast pocket. Birdie grinned and settled down, and the second miracle of Lourdes happened right there in Grandma Ada's parlor. She counted a measure, gave Birdie a nod, and they were off. He didn't miss a beat. The hand that couldn't guide a pencil or color inside the lines played those spoons like a pro and had the relatives all clapping before the first few measures were finished. Glumly, I thought for a minute that they might actually get up and polka right there in the parlor, even knowing that Grandma believed that dancing, drinking, and playing cards, except for old maid or rook, were the work of the devil.

When the polka ended with a "shave and a haircut, two bits!" Grandma Ada whirled around on her stool and gave Birdie the biggest hug of his life. Marion pounded him on the back and proudly announced, "Hey, looks like we've got another musician in the family. Atta boy, Bird!" My mother and father were positively beaming.

I thought my misery was finally at end when Grandma closed the piano and said, "Best put out a little lunch before the men folk have to get home to their chores." She sent Grandpa to fetch a jar of dills from the cellar and hustled into the kitchen to make sandwiches out of the turkey leftovers while my mother set out the pie plates, the remaining blueberry, apple, and pumpkin pastry divided into tiny wedges to give everyone at least a taste. Great-grandma Mary Ellen stirred an egg into fresh Folgers grounds for the boiled coffee. The men waited in the living room and discussed whether or not the weather would hold until the corn picking was done. "Be a damn shame if we can't git it all out," Cousin William said, shaking his head and lowering his voice so his blasphemy wouldn't carry into the kitchen. "God knows it'd be nice to go into spring plantin' with a little extra cash in the pocket for a change." That was a good one. My father said Uncle William was loaded, probably still had the first nickel he ever made and would for sure take his pile of dough with him when he took the big dirt nap sometime down the road.

* * *

Alas, it was not to be—the end to my misery, that is. The week after Thanksgiving, Dad came home from Worthington with a ukulele. My father was one of those fortunate souls who could pick up almost anything and get some music out of it: a comb wrapped in waxed paper, a blade of canary grass, or a hand-whittled tuner. "What d'ya think, Ruthie?" he asked as he tuned the four strings to "My Dog Has Fleas,"—G, C, D, and A—tightening and loosening the pegs until he was satisfied. Then he strummed and sang "You Are My Sunshine."

My mother just shook her head and asked, "How much did that thing cost?"

Birdie was utterly fascinated. Since his musical debut in Grandma's parlor, he was never without two spoons in his front shirt pocket. The kids in school had a great time during recess making sport of it. They'd grab the spoons and use them to rap him on the top of his head before tossing them in the dirt. And it would be a serious under-statement to say our teacher was just a bit unhappy with Birdie's spoons, but then she hit upon the idea of sending him to the basement during afternoon reading time to see if the janitor needed any help and said he could stay down there and practice his spoons until dismissal time.

Birdie was out the door before she could change her mind, anything to escape the boredom of coloring and the constant admonition to "Stay in the lines, Birdie." I liked the arrangement, too, because it saved the torment and embarrassment of listening to Birdie struggle through even a sentence. But when my mother found out about Birdie's daily time in the janitor's mop room, she hit the roof. My father usually went to the basement after supper to clean the eggs we'd gathered during the evening chores with a soft rag dipped in diluted vinegar. It magically removed any chicken poop without much rubbing. I helped sometimes, especially if it got me out of scrubbing the pots and pans. But that night, my mother followed us downstairs.

"What's goin' on, Ruthie?" my father asked, settling down on a wobbly chair near the egg crate.

My mother didn't waste words. "How's Birdie supposed to learn to read sitting down in the mop room with Warren every afternoon, Job? Tell me that."

"Don't hear Birdie complainin' about it, Ruthie."

It was not the response my mother was looking for, and she let my father have it. "You really don't care, do you, Job? It's just fine with you if he never learns to read." She turned and stormed back up the stairs, her voice trembling with anger and tears. "You've never cared, Job. Admit it! You've never cared."

My father just kept cleaning the eggs. "I care, Ruthie, just as much as you do, but I know when to stop expectin' things that won't ever be."

The next morning, my mother drove to school and put an end to Birdie's time in the mop room, but not much happened on the reading end of things, and Miss Gannon didn't seem to like Birdie and me as much as before.

It wasn't long before Birdie added the ukulele to his musical repertoire. He had an ear for it, my father said. I guess that must have been the reason he spent so much time tuning the stupid uke. He was forever doing the "My Dog Has Fleas" thing, loosening and tightening the strings until at least one invariably snapped. Dad finally got a little cross about it. "Quit tunin' the damn thing and just play it, Bird!"

* * *

At the end of every six-week marking period, Miss Gannon's class celebrated with a class party. She furnished the Watkins orangeade, and we took turns bringing cookies. Besides the treats, we had a little program, a show-and-tell time. So far, these afternoon soirees had been mostly "show"—that is to say, vocal, piano, and trumpet solos, except for Buzz Carlson, who always brought a dead animal wrapped in a gunnysack and told how he'd trapped and killed it and then showed how to skin it. Miss Gannon tolerated his first demonstration because the poor critter was a squirrel, and it didn't take Buzz more than a couple of minutes to slit the legs and peel the pelt away.

But when he pulled a skunk out of his sack the next time, she had an absolute cow. Buzz was pretty cool about it, though. "It's okay, Miss Gannon," he said, "I pulled the stinker out at home." Actually, Buzz's labs were usually the best part of the party and didn't seem to keep anyone from enjoying the treats, except for Miss Gannon, who just sipped on the orangeade anyway. It was good for Buzz, too, because it was the only time he got much attention from the class or teacher. It's funny how he never got any gold stars on his science papers, but still ended up being a biology professor at Iowa State.

When Miss Gannon announced the last party of the year, she encouraged the students who hadn't shared a talent thus far to think about what they could do. "It is part of your participation grade," she explained. I don't think for one minute our teacher had Birdie in mind, but he had other ideas. "I'm gonna take Dad's uke and play 'You Are My Sunshine' for the kids, Ivy May," he said, clapping his hands in excitement. "I bet they'll think I'm pretty good, Ivy May. I bet they will . . . bet they will. Bet they'll think it's pretty swell to play a uke, Ivy May. Bet they will."

I covered my ears and hollered, "Stop saying it over and over! I heard you the first time, Birdie. I hate it when you do that!"

It was a horrible idea, but my mother said Birdie had just as much right to play the ukulele as Buzz Carlson had to bring roadkill to school. The problem was, she didn't know half of what went on at school, and I didn't tell her because I knew it would just make her mad or sad. I hadn't forgotten Marion's warning. Miss Gannon called on Birdie last. I think she was hoping we'd run out of time. No such luck. Birdie took the ukulele out of the pillowcase my mother had used to protect it from being scratched and started tuning the four strings to "My Dog Has Fleas."

"What's he doin'?" Kenny Zaph hollered out. "Hey, Birdie, you got fleas?" And then Kenny scratched his underarms and made sounds like a monkey. Miss Gannon tried unsuccessfully to squelch the laughter, but it was to no avail. Birdie laughed, too, because he didn't have the sense to know they were laughing at him, not with him. He never did get to sing "You Are My Sunshine." Miss Gannon said the party was over, and we could get our coats and play outside until the bus came. Birdie and I were last on, and the entire bus sang out in unison, "Birdie's got fleas!" It hadn't taken long for Kenny Zaph to do his dirty work.

After the bus dropped us off that afternoon, Marion raced up the lane and waited for me by the yard gate. "Stop cryin' and wipe the snot off your face, Ivy May. Mom'll know somethin's wrong. Remember what I said before. Keep your mouth shut.

I pushed him aside. "It's Wednesday, so she's at Ladies Aid, but I'm telling when she gets home."

"All you ever do is tattle, Ivy May. No wonder you only got one friend, and she's a drip."

* * *

After supper dishes were done, Birdie disappeared to get Dad's uke from the top of the piano in the front room and began his nonstop tuning. Mom set up the ironing board, and I worked at the kitchen table, writing my weekly spelling words over three times while Marion finished his long-division problems. "I don't see why she makes us prove every answer," he grumbled. "There's fifty of these stupid things we have to do, and I've never got one wrong yet."

My mother dipped her fingers in a nearby saucer of warm water, shook them over the dress she was pressing, and looked at Marion. "Well, it's good practice, Marion. Don't complain about something that's good for you."

"It's just dumb busywork, that's all."

"Marion," my father called from the dining room where he was reading the *Globe*, "Stop the arguin' and finish your work. And, Birdie, quit that infernal tunin' and play somethin'!"

Then my mother remembered. "Oh, Birdie, I forgot to ask," she said, stepping into the front room. "How did it go today, Birdie? Did the kids like your playing?" Marion kicked me hard under the table and bent his head over his long division.

"We got out early, so I didn't git to play. The kids thought it was real funny when I tuned it, though. They all laughed. They all laughed real hard."

"Hey, Birdie," my father interrupted, "how about I chord on the piano while you strum along?"

Mom came back to finish her ironing without saying a word. Finally, I asked, "Can you give me my words, Mom?"

"Of course, Ivy May. Then you need to get to bed." Then she cleared her throat. "I guess I need to wipe my nose a bit first."

* * *

The next morning, Kenny did an earthshaking thing. He sat with Birdie and me. I thought maybe he was going to be nice for a change when he put his arm around Birdie, but then he said, "Still got fleas, Birdie? Want some help scratchin'?" Then he grabbed Birdie's hat, threw it to the back of the bus and did his monkey routine again. "My Dog Has Fleas" became bully fodder for the next month.

Getting Involved

My father was into community involvement big time. He was a joiner with a special fondness for elevator co-ops. Mom often grumbled he was forever on the lookout for some committee that might be a member short. The only time she remembered his balking was when Cousin Lenora invited him to be a part of the Osceola chapter of the Ku Klux Klan. "There aren't any black folks in the county right now, but some could always move in from Sioux City," she warned, "and it never hurts to keep an eye on those Irish Catholics and the other riffraff."

The invitation came on a postcard with Lenora's family pictured on the front, dressed in full Klan regalia. The message on the back in her fine Palmer Method script read, "A 100% American family. In these white robes the world knows we stand for God, Home, and Country." In my mother's estimation, they were mighty silly words coming from a self-righteous old woman who bragged about her Tory roots. Mom shook her head in disgust. "Egad! I told your father to give me that dreadful thing, and I lifted the front lid of the cook stove and burned it on the spot. I'm just thankful John must not have had time to read everybody's mail that day or else the whole countryside would have known."

* * *

When I was eight, Dad decided it was high time that Birdie, Marion, and I got involved in 4-H. Mom agreed it would be a good thing for the three of us. It was pretty hard to find fault with an organization that asked each member to pledge head to clearer thinking, heart to greater loyalty, hands to larger service, and health to better living for club, community, and country. Munger farm kids either joined the Go-Getters or the Indian Lake Progressives, depending on the side of the county line on which they lived. Our farm was on the Nobles County side, so we pledged our heads, hearts, hands, and health once a month with the Progressives.

Back then, it was pretty much a given that every 4-Her would have a livestock project—raise and show some kind of critter. Even a lop-eared rabbit or a fancy rooster would do, but a baby beef project was the hands-down favorite and easily the most prestigious. A Hereford, Angus, or Shorthorn with a big purple ribbon draped over its neck at fair judging time was front-page stuff in the *Globe*. The competition for this honor was fierce. Fathers went shopping out of state to find a spring calf, wide in the hind end and deep in the withers, that would fatten up over the winter and spring on some extra shelled corn dribbled with a little molasses and sport just the right layer of finish come August and the Nobles County Fair.

Always pragmatic, my father argued the object of the project wasn't to raise a show calf, but to learn how to raise good quality beef economically; thus, our calves came out of the Ames herd. The two Herford calves Dad singled out for Marion and Birdie when he weaned that fall were pretty nice, but mine not only looked wild-eyed and bloody from his dehorning and castration the day before, but also on the scrawny side, even to my inexperienced eyes. Our neighbor Emil Froeling thought so, too. "I don't know, Job . . ." he said, looking over the three penned calves with us. "Two of 'em look like they'll feed out okay, but that one you picked out for Ivy May don't look like it'll amount to much." Emil winked at me, so I knew something good was about to come down the pike. It was one of those times when looking woebegone had an up side. "Ivy's gotta have somethin' better than that for her first calf." I think he remembered me shivering in my undies in Grandma Ada's kitchen that first day of town school and felt sorry for the poor little Ames girl, about to get the short end of the stick again.

"She can have mine if she wants," Birdie volunteered. I don't think the idea of leading around what would become a thousand-pound steer sounded all that wonderful to him. I wasn't really enthralled either. It made my heart fibrillate just to think about it.

"Why does Ivy May even get to have a baby beef project?" Marion asked. "She should sign up for food preparation or somethin' for girls." Then he punched my arm. "I'm tellin' you right now, Drippy, I'm not feedin' your calf. You can get your butt out of bed in the morning and do it yourself."

"Oh, shut up!" I stuck my tongue out and moved closer

to Emil, certain at that moment that I absolutely did want a calf, just to spite Marion.

Usually Dad ignored our squabbles, but not this time. "Hey," he scolded, "that's no way to talk to your little sister."

"Well, if Ivy May gets Birdie's calf, then I'm done with 4-H."

"Guess that's up to you, Marion," my father said.

"You know, Job, I just might have the ticket. Remember that heifer that died when we pulled her calf? I've been bottle feedin' the little guy ever since. Kinda turned into a damn pet, following me around the cow yard ... can hardly chase it away, it's so friendly. Be perfect for Ivy May." He squeezed me to his side. "Whatcha think, Toots?"

"You'd better ask Emil what he wants for it, Ivy May. Don't think he's givin' it away."

"I was thinkin' around fifty bucks, Job."

Dad looked at me and nodded. "I'll take it," I said, feeling important to be in on a big business decision like that. Emil shook hands on the deal and stepped out of the barn to roll a cigarette and shoot the breeze with my father about dredging the ditch while I ran to the house for the checkbook.

"What's your father buying now?" my mother asked. She took the checkbook out of the top drawer of the cupboard and thumbed through the stubs to find the balance before handing it to me.

"I'm gettin' a real good calf for 4-H." I grabbed the checkbook and ran back to the barn.

"Wanna go git your calf right now, Ivy May? Might as well." Emil whistled for Rex, the big Airedale that always rode shotgun, rain or shine. The dog came on the run, panting heavily from the exertion of wildly barking and chasing my mother's irate laying hens around the chicken house. I knew she'd have a few words about it at supper time. She claimed it caused blood spots in the egg yolks, but Dad said that had more to do with the old rooster than Rex. Emil stepped on the running board and told me to jump in. "Ride in the back with Rex if you want, Ivy May."

"Can Birdie come, too?"

"You bet . . . always got room for Birdie."

Marion stood there looking like he'd been weaned on a pickle as we circled the dooryard and headed down the lane. His sour puss assured me it was well worth getting up fifteen minutes earlier in the morning and smelling like barn instead of pancakes when I climbed on the school bus. I figured I couldn't stink worse than the Mallorys. They reeked of fried fish for the whole six weeks of Lent.

* * *

I named my calf Snoopy, even when Dad shook his head and said it wasn't a good idea. "Some time down the road he's gonna end up hamburger and some nice T-bones, Ivy May. It's just city folks that think everything's gotta have a name." Marion barked and said Snoopy sounded like a dog's name.

"Who cares?" I shot back. "He's not your calf."

* * *

By early August, Snoopy was huge, close to eleven hundred pounds, mostly due to his greedy behavior at feeding time. He was smart enough to figure out that if he stood sideways at feed bunk instead of head-in, he prevented Birdie and Marion's calves from even getting their noses in the ground corn, much less their fair share of it. Snoopy would efficiently work his way down the bunk, leaving only a handful for the other two to fight over. Then he moved on to freshly busted bales and enjoyed the fragrant alfalfa without any competition. Emil dropped over at least once a week to check on his bottle baby. "Lookin' good, Ivy May," he'd say. But as the county fair drew nearer, he started saying worrisome things like "Hope he ain't gonna be too big for Ivy May handle, Job." I was petrified at the thought.

"Nah," my father said. "He's as tame as they come. She'll do fine."

"I'm not helpin'," Marion said. "It's her project."

The Sunday before the opening day of the Nobles County Fair, Dad invited Grandpa Henry and Grandma Ada out for fried spring chicken, corn on the cob, green apple pie, and front-row seats on the west lawn for the grand preparation of our baby beef projects. The steers needed a good scrubbing and currying before we loaded them in the truck for the trip to Worthington the following morning. Marion haltered his steer first, and Dad helped tie its head close and tight to the big gate post so there wouldn't be any way the calf could kick up his heels, even if he got the notion, without choking himself. Then he backed away for Marion to step up with the bucket of water. "Get 'im a little acquainted with the water first, Marion. Just dip your brush in the pail and move slow as you work on his hind quarter." Marion got right to work and, except for a few blats, his calf was cooperative.

"Nothin' to it, Ivy May," he offered snidely as he put his calf back in the pen.

Mom went in the house and came back with the coffeepot so she could refill Grandma and Grandpa's cups while Dad led Birdie's calf out. "Your turn," he hollered to Birdie, who was peeking around the corner of the garage. When he didn't move, Dad hollered again, "Come on, Bird. Let's go." He was using his no-nonsense tone of voice, and Birdie knew it. He came slowly, scuffing his shoes in the loose dirt, and stood a safe distance from the steer. "Move in on 'im, Bird. You can't do nothin' standin' back there." My father shoved the pail in Birdie's hand and pulled him forward. My mother went into her frantic mode. "Job, can't you see he's scared to death?"

My father's response was immediate and cross. "Stop babyin' him, Ruthie!" He's twelve years old, woman. If he can drive a tractor, he sure as hell can step up here and put a brush in the bucket." I didn't see the connection.

The steer seemed docile enough until Birdie forgot Dad's admonition to get him used to the water gradually. Instead, he heaved the whole bucket of cold, soapy well water and hit the steer right between the eyes. The once-tame beast gave a terrified blat, rolled his eyes back wildly, and began bucking like a rodeo bull, his fear changing in an instant to crazed fury as he contorted his half-ton body until he somehow mounted the gatepost. His torn belly balanced for a second on the top of it before the old piece of fencing snapped in two and sent him toppling on his back. Dad grabbed the lead rope, which was still attached to the broken half of the post, before the steer could scramble to his feet. From there, things went south in a big hurry. All the while trying to keep his grip on the rope, my father ended up underneath Birdie's steer, rolling over on his stomach to protect his face from the shower of blood, butting head, and slashing hooves. Birdie dropped his bucket and ran for the house. Marion ducked into the granary. Mom dropped the coffeepot, and she and Grandma Ada turned into a couple of wailing banshees, which did nothing to improve the steer's disposition. I did my part by throwing up three ears of sweet corn over by the catalpa tree.

It was Grandpa Henry who saved Dad from being trampled. "Let go of the damn rope, Job!" he yelled and ran at the steer, shouting and waving his arms to distract him. Then he headed toward the open barn door with the berserk animal in angry pursuit. From the awful commotion in the barn, we all thought Grandpa was a goner until he came around the side of the barn, carrying the pint of Jim Beam he kept in the tack room. "Think I need a good nip," he said, downing what was left in the pint in one gulp.

The sideshow was over, Snoopy's bath forgotten. Mom and Grandma Ada helped Dad get his battered, bruised body into the house after he shed his manure- and blood-covered overalls in the porch. The bawling and thudding continued in the barn. Grandpa said the crazy bastard was head-butting the cement wall, and it wouldn't be long before he broke his neck. "Might as well call the renderin' works to come in the mornin', Job," he advised.

The steer was still rampaging at nightfall. Finally, my father took his gun from the corner of the entryway and headed for the barn. "You kids stay in the house with your mother." The four of us huddled in the kitchen and listened for the sharp crack of the rifle and the silence that followed it.

I fell asleep thinking Birdie was lucky. He could still go to the fair and have fun without dragging a steer around.

* * *

Emil was over bright and early the next morning to load our calves, along with bales of straw and alfalfa, a gunny-sack of shelled corn, a bucket for water, and halters, curry-combs and brushes for the three-day affair. My mother had a new pair of jeans and a five-dollar bill laid out for each of us in the downstairs bedroom. "Don't spend it on soda, and stay away from the carnival stands," she warned. "They're not clean. Goodness knows where those people have had their hands. Get a sloppy joe and glass of milk at the Bethlehem Lutheran booth. Their Ladies Aid always has good home cooking, none of that awful stuff that's been deep-fried in rancid oil. And stay off the rides. Down in Iowa someplace last year, a bucket fell off the Ferris wheel and killed two boys."

"Good God, Ruthie," my father laughed. "Quit your stewin'. The kids'll be fine."

I chose that moment to make a last ditch attempt to stay home. "I feel like throwin' up," I whimpered, holding my mouth with one hand and my stomach with the other. It didn't work.

"You're just fakin' it, Ivy May," Marion scoffed. Behind my father's back, he mouthed, "Baby, baby!"

Dad shook his head. "Git in the car, you kids, and quit your squabblin'. We gotta be at the fairgrounds before Emil gets there with the steers."

My mother followed us to the car. "Marion, you keep an eye on Birdie and Ivy May. Don't be running off with your friends. Remember, your sister's just a little girl." Marion slid into the front seat muttering that was the reason I shouldn't have a baby beef project. I was wondering myself why I hadn't opted to make half a dozen cupcakes and hang out in the food building with Dorie Ann instead of sitting on a straw bale in the livestock barn.

I was sure of it when we unloaded our calves at the livestock barn. "Get outta the way, kid," somebody hollered. I scooted to the side, stepped in a fresh cow pie, and turned to see a Holstein bull, topping off at a ton or more, barreling down the runway, his only restraint a huge nose ring and a determined dairy farmer with a death grip on the attached chain. It was a good thing I was wearing my new jeans. At least nobody could see the pee run down my leg. But that wasn't the half of it. Our assigned stalls were on the east side of the barn, so we had to pass through the rotunda, around and behind gigantic Belgians and Clydesdales being settled in, and several more angry bulls. It was the near-death experience of my formative years.

Dad went home to weed the beans in the peat ground after we stalled our steers. The baby-beef judging wasn't until the following afternoon, so we had time on our hands. Marion immediately ran off with some kids he knew from Brewster . . . so much for keeping an eye on his little sister.

Finally I said, "Let's go get a grape Nehi, Birdie."

"Then can we look at the tractors?" he asked. I nodded. Even admiring a few Olivers and dump rakes sounded good to me right then. "You still gotta lotta cow poop on your one shoe, Ivy May," he said as we walked toward the midway. "Some's on your sock, too."

By early afternoon, Birdie and I were back, sitting on a hay bale behind our steers. The barn supervisor, an old geezer named Bill who patrolled the alleyways and forked a little poop over to the side now and then, was back and forth a few times before he decided to stop and have a little fun with us. He used the crook of his cane to snare Birdie's ankle and pull him off the bale to land on his behind. "Gotcha now," he teased.

"Stop it!" I said weakly. Bill leaned toward me and cupped his ear.

"Whatcha say, honey?"

I found my mother in me in that moment. "I'm not your honey. And stop teasing my brother."

"Oh, I'm just havin' a little fun with 'im." He caught

Birdie's ankle again and jerked hard. "He don't seem bothered none. See how he's laughin'?"

"Stop it or I'll tell my dad!"

Birdie, giggling uncontrollably by this time, scrambled to his feet and ran at Bill, who stepped aside, hooked him once again, this time behind the knee, and sent him tumbling face forward into the muck of the alleyway. "Try to get me again. Betcha can't," Birdie hollered.

"Whoa now! That's enough. We're makin' your little sister cry. I'll tell you what, though. How about grabbin' a fork and helpin' me pick up a few cow pies?" And just like that, Birdie was gone, and it was just Ivy May Ames sitting there on the bale, wiping tears and a runny nose with the back of her hand and hating both her brothers.

It wasn't long before Marion showed up without his pals and carrying a Kewpie doll. "Where's Birdie?" he asked.

"He ran off to help Bill pick up cow pies even after Bill was mean to him," I choked out between sobs. "And I'm tellin' Mom on both of you, Marion. I don't care what you say about not makin' her sad. People pick on Birdie all the time, and he thinks they're just havin' fun. You should've been here to help. Mom told you to, Marion."

"Stop cryin', Ivy May. I'll go find Birdie and we'll do somethin' fun. Maybe we can put our money together and go see Joey Chitwood in the grandstand."

* * *

Watching Joey Chitwood was not my idea of a swell time. Marion had spent all of his money winning that stupid

Kewpie doll, so Birdie and I had to pay his admission. Dust and noise, that's all it was. Joey catapulted his demolition buggy off a ramp to jump first one car, then two, and finally three. The crowd roared in appreciation as he came to a screeching halt in front of the grandstand, jumped out of his car, doffed his helmet, and took a sweeping bow. Next he went for a Guinness world record. He drove by the grandstand at breakneck speed several times, balancing his car on its two side wheels just a little longer each time. The crowd went nuts and screamed when he finally ended up upside down, all four wheels spinning in the air. Marion and Birdie were caught up in the excitement. I was ready to go back to my bale in the livestock barn.

* * *

The next day made up for everything. For one thing, Birdie didn't go to the fair. When I told my mother about Bill and how Birdie and Marion ran off and left me, she scolded Marion and decided that Birdie should probably just drop out of 4-H and stay home if folks were going to make fun of him. That meant that when the judging was over, I could hang out with Dorie Ann. She didn't like it much when Birdie tagged along.

The judging started in early afternoon. Emil came in time to show me how to curry and brush my steer to make his butt look as wide as possible. "Keep his head up, Ivy May, and tap him under the belly so he don't look swaybacked." Emil's advice was for naught. It was a hot, humid day, and all Snoopy wanted to do was lie down and chew his cud. Finally, my dad grabbed a cattle prod from someone and gave my steer a good jolt in the hinder, and I pulled him in line. Emil's bottle-fed baby came through with flying colors, reserve champion overall, and I got a purple ribbon and my picture in the *Daily Globe.*

Afterwards, I ran to find Dorie Ann in the food building, and we had a good laugh when we saw the white ribbon on LuAnn Miller's cupcakes. They were flat as pancakes.

The End of Summer

My father always said that farming was pretty much a crap shoot, dependent on the possibility of early planting; the absence of crop pests—corn bore, smut, blight, and the like; adequate rain, not too much or little; a late, dry fall to safeguard against an early killing frost and insure a timely harvest; and, ultimately, the market. Ironically, none of these was something Job Ames or his farm neighbors could control, yet they persevered and celebrated the simple gifts of a good summer sod-soaker and a blooming flax field, all the while keeping their fingers crossed that the dredge ditch wouldn't overflow or a straight wind out of the northwest flatten the grain.

In the middle of July, with the oats standing tall and beginning to head out, my father felt safe in selling off the rest of last year's oats crop, binned in the clandestine play corner of the haymow since the previous summer. Besides making room for the new crop, which promised a good yield, it would put a little much-needed cash in the checking account at Farmer's State to tide us over until the feedlot steers were shipped off in late August to the Sioux City Stockyard. So with oats up from sixty-five to seventy cents a bushel, my father made the move. "Birdie," he said that Tuesday morning at breakfast. "How about takin' a load of oats to town?" Birdie was fourteen and, by that time, my father's right-hand man. He wasn't thrilled about slopping the pigs, pitching manure, or picking rocks, but he was Johnny-on-the-spot when it came to driving the tractor for any reason at all, and he did it well. Grandpa Henry scratched his head in puzzlement, saying he couldn't get over how somebody who couldn't spell his own name was able to handle a tractor like he'd been born to it. Birdie drove the John Deere, sitting tall and proud and raising his hand in greeting to anyone who might happen to be around as he drove through the dooryard or along the gravel road to a nearby field. And, amazingly, he even quickly mastered the difficult feat of backing a four-wheeled grain wagon into the granary alleyway without having to take a second stab at it, something Dad and his farm neighbors couldn't always do. In his work around the farm, Birdie found that sense of personal worth, within easy reach of most of us but so elusive for folks who are reminded daily they don't measure up.

Birdie jumped at my father's offer of new responsibility. His tractor driving hadn't extended beyond our dooryard and farm fields, so the thought of actually taking a load of grain into town was heart-stopping to him. His grin said it all. "Sure," he said, and he grabbed one of the dozen or so free caps from the DeKalb seed-corn salesman piled in the corner of the entryway and took off at a trot, hollering back, "I'll back 'er up to the barn." My father returned to his pancakes and *Sioux City Journal*, waiting, I knew, for my mother's outburst. It came quickly. She dropped the hot griddle into the kitchen sink, causing the dishwater to explode into a cloud of steam, and rounded on my father.

"Have you lost your mind, Job?" she said, her lips flattening across her teeth in anger. "Driving on our place is one thing, but letting Birdie go into town by himself is downright asinine!"

"Who said anything about him goin' alone?" my father asked, shaking out the paper as he found the farm market section. "Marion and Ivy May can ride along on top of the load. Get 'em out of your hair for a while." He pushed back from the table, stood up, and dug deep in his side pocket for change. "Here's a couple quarters. You kids can stop at Mel's and get a root beer float after you unload." He handed them to Marion, and then stepped behind my mother, who had turned back to the sink and the windows above it to watch as Birdie cranked the flywheel of the John Deere. My father pushed aside a few errant strands of auburn hair that had fallen from her bun and kissed the back of her neck before saying, "You gotta stop your nonstop worryin', Ruthie. It don't help a thing, except make Birdie feel more worthless that he already does. That what you want?"

"Oh, stop that!" My mother swatted his hand away and turned to face him. She wasn't ready to surrender her argument. "Weren't you just complaining the other day that the shoulders of the road were soft and the township had better get busy and do a little grading before someone goes in the ditch?"

My father shook his head and laughed as he headed for the door, "You never forget a damn thing when it suits your way of thinkin', do you, Ruthie?" Marion and I followed close on his heels, lest we be denied a trip into town and a float at Mel's.

Birdie had the wagon backed up to the barn, and it didn't take long for my father to let down the chute of the mow bin to release a steady stream of oats. The four-wheeler filled quickly, but not before my father frowned and reached into the flow of grain to retrieve a red cap. And before Marion could shake his head to warn him, Birdie blurted out, "There it is! I knew we'd find it, Marion." Then he clapped his hand over his mouth and looked down at his scuffed shoes, suddenly aware of what he'd said.

My father waited until the oats were reduced to a trickle before he said, "If you wanna be in that bin so bad, Marion and Ivy May, git your hind ends up there and shovel what's left in the corners over to the chute." We scrambled up the ladder and into the bin, the past allure quickly lost in the suffocating heat and dusty air thick with oat chaff.

"I can't breathe, Marion!" I cried. "I gotta get out!"

"Oh, shut up, Ivy May! It's just your claustrophobia. You can breathe. You're just talkin' yourself into a fit." Marion was in love with the phobia words he'd learned in a sixth-grade vocabulary lesson and was always quick to flaunt his newfound knowledge. He said it explained why I got so crazy when he shut me in the closet or put the pillow over my head for even a second.

My mother was still miffed when we drove out of the dooryard, Marion and I atop the load. She walked to the orchard clothesline with her clothesbasket of wet sheets without even a backward glance at us. Heading toward the pig barn, my father hollered one last admonition. "Keep your eye on the road, Birdie, and stay off the shoulder. And Marion, don't forget to pick up the receipt from Alvin." We turned south out of the driveway and up onto the gravel road, the load shifting as we hit a deep pothole still storing muddy water from a previous downpour. Marian and I burrowed down in the oats to enjoy the summer day. The breeze was fresh, the morning sun bright in a cloudless blue sky, and there was the promise of a root beer float soon to be satisfied.

After a half mile, we were over the knoll, out of sight of the farm, and passing Shady Nook, which was already showing signs of neglect—weeds reaching the boarded windows, the outhouse tipped over by a Halloween prankster, and swings hanging haphazardly by single ropes. Marion was suddenly quiet. I wondered if he was remembering the time during recess when we made a game out of jumping over the sharp stumps of newly axed saplings in the school grove. We weren't supposed to leave the mowed area around the school, but we often did. Miss Fiola was never the wiser as she stood around the corner talking to her boyfriend, who always stopped by on his daily trips into town. Marion was a good jumper and a bit of a show-off. He knew he was playing to an audience of admiring schoolmates. He cleared all of the stumps easily, his face red with exertion and excitement, and expressed disappointment when the recess bell rang before he could attempt one last jump. As we ran back to the school, Marion told his fan club, "Hang around after school, and I'll jump the whole row of 'em without stoppin'."

Usually everybody, including Miss Fiola, took off for home right after the last bell, and that afternoon was no exception. Nobody showed up to watch Marion except Birdie and me. "Well, I'm gonna try it anyway," he said. "I'll take a practice run and show the kids tomorrow at recess."

Dropping his books, Marion took off his jacket, knelt on one knee, eyed the row of sharp stumps, and then sprang forward, cleanly hurdling six stumps without slowing, but suddenly losing his balance when his trailing foot caught on a wild grapevine, leaving him literally impaled on the next sapling. There was a loud rip, and Marion fell forward, clutching his crotch as blood ran between fingers and spread down the pants leg of his bib overalls.

I heard Birdie scream, but it sounded far away. Then he sobbed, "Do somethin', Ivy May, You gotta do somethin'! Marion's gonna die! His blood's all comin' out!" The only thing I could think of doing was to run to the outhouse and come back with giant wads of toilet paper. Marion shoved it down his overalls and pressed hard to staunch the flow of blood. After a while it seemed like the bleeding had stopped, but when he tried to stand, it spurted again. I ran for more toilet paper. Birdie took off for home at a dead run. "I'm gonna git the wagon, Ivy May, and pull him home. Ma's at Ladies Aid. She won't even know."

A fine sheen of perspiration covered Marion's white face as he nodded and closed his eyes. I sank down on my knees beside him and promised God that I would never say another mean word about LuAnne Miller if Marion didn't die there in the Shady Nook grove. It seemed forever before Birdie was back with the coaster wagon and an old blanket from the garage. We helped Marion up to sit sideways in the wagon, lifted his legs over, and started the half mile home, Birdie and me both pulling. I don't know how Marion did it, but he sat up the whole way, one hand holding on to the side of the wagon and the other pressed against his crotch.

Relieved that the garage was still empty and there was no sign of my father, we helped Marion into the house and up the stairs to the bedroom he and Birdie shared. "Get some more toilet paper, Ivy May," he said and then shut the door in my face. I raced to the outhouse and came back with the extra roll my mother always stashed in the corner on top of the Montgomery Ward catalog. Marion opened the door just enough to reach a bloody hand through and grasp the paper.

The rest is a blur. Birdie hollered, "Ma's home!" and we tumbled down the stairs. My mother met us on the bottom step, holding the bloody blanket from the wagon. She pushed us aside on her way up, taking two steps at a time, and I heard the door slam open against the wall before she screamed and staggered back down the stairs, carrying my brother in her arms. God's eye was truly on the sparrow that day, because He chose that exact moment to have our neighbor Emil Froehling stop over to deliver a couple of pails of pickling cucumbers. He grabbed Marion from my mother and lifted him onto the front seat of his pickup, boosted my mother in beside him, and took off for Worthington, laying on the horn to alert my father, who was digging out a badger den in the west alfalfa field.

It wasn't long before Dad thundered into the dooryard, the stone boat tipped upside down and dragging on its underside as he urged the horses on and finally pulled them to a stop.

"What's goin' on?" he shouted over the blowing team. "I saw Emil take off down the road like a bat outta hell." Birdie and I just stood there, mute. My father looked around and frowned before asking, "Cat got your tongues? Where's Marion and your mother?"

"She went with," Birdie answered and then looked at me to fill in the details.

"Marion was jumping over the stumps in the school grove and . . ." My voice trailed off in embarrassment as I remembered his bloody pants.

"Damn!" my father swore. "Don't you kids know better than to do a darn fool thing like that?" When there was no answer, he pushed his cap back on his head and sighed. "The both of you . . . git in the house and stay outta trouble while I put the team away."

Birdie and I went in and sat at the kitchen table. I wasn't hungry, but Birdie ate four chocolate chip cookies. "Is Marion dead?" he asked.

Later, when Emil brought Marion and my mother home, my father stayed outside for a few minutes to visit. I watched and listened through the screen door as Emil took time to roll a cigarette before he lowered his voice and said, "Yep, good thing I was bringing over those cukes, Job. The kid damn near castrated himself."

* * *

"Marion," I said, breaking the silence, "do you think you got castrated that day after school when you were jumpin' over the tree stumps?"

"You don't even know what you're talkin' about, Ivy May."

"I do too. I've seen Dad do it to the pigs."

"Well, I'm no pig, Ivy May," Marion shouted. He grabbed a handful of oats and threw it, hitting me squarely in the face, and soon the seriousness of the past minutes turned to fun as we used both hands to pelt each other with oats. What happened next was the "if only" of the rest of my life. Marion motioned for me to follow him as he crawled forward to the front of the wagon. "On the count of three," he yelled, "let's get Birdie." We both fired fistfuls of oats as hard as we could. Our aim was perfect as we hit Birdie squarely in the back of the head, neck, and shoulders. He took one hand off the steering wheel to ward off the next assault and turned around to grin at us.

In those brief seconds, the wagon veered off onto the soft shoulder and started to tip, its heavy load bearing it down. The tongue broke loose from the tractor hitch and the wagon pitched sideways, spilling some of its oats before it landed bottom-up, wheels spinning, in the deep ditch. I was thrown against the barbed-wire fence, and from there I watched Birdie jump from the tractor and run down the road for home. I couldn't see Marion. He was buried somewhere in the load of oats.

I was ten years old, and I thought if I pounded on the side of the wagon, Marion would hear me and know that everything was going to be alright. I pounded and pounded, unaware of gathering neighbors and the clanking of tow chains, until Grandpa Henry pulled me away and carried me to the car. As the door closed, I heard Emil Froehling say, ". . . probably tried to ride the wagon down and got sucked into the oats" and Inez Benson, standing close along the side of the road so she wouldn't miss anything, put in her two cents, as usual. "Somthin' was bound to happen, lettin' that Birdie drive the tractor all over creation. My word! What were Job and Ruthie thinkin', anyway?"

* * *

Grandma Ada was already in the kitchen, busying herself over by the sink as she pumped water into the coffeepot. My mother was sitting at the table, looking straight ahead, her body motionless except for her hands, which were busy smoothing the oilcloth and tracing the pattern of red and yellow fruit over and over. She didn't even glance at Grandpa when he looked at Grandma and shook his head, or at me when she asked, "Ivy May, have you practiced your piano lesson today?" There was no sign of Birdie.

Grandma took one look at me, put the pot down, and said with false cheerfulness, "Come over here to the sink, Ivy May. Let's git you cleaned up a bit. My goodness! You're a sight for sore eyes. Where's your brother?"

When I didn't answer, Grandpa said, "Oh, Birdie's around here someplace, probably hidin' in the barn. He'll show up sooner or later."

* * *

Then we waited in the deep silence that comes with the helpless sense of impending doom. Grandma Ada sat in the kitchen with my mother, and Grandpa took me into the living room. He kept his eyes on the bay window. When he suddenly started and cleared his throat, I looked up in time to see Benson's black hearse with its tinted windows pass by on the road. It wasn't long before my father drove the tractor into the driveway and parked down by the machine shed, but he didn't come in. Finally, Grandpa put on his cap and went out. My mother was suddenly alert.

As if to keep out the bad news, she got up quickly, went to the door, and pushed the dead bolt home before moving on to pull the café curtains over the sink window. Then she returned to the table and her tracing. It wasn't long before Grandpa Henry was at the locked door with Dad. Grandma Ada started to get up, but my mother covered her hand with hers and shook her head. My father pushed Grandpa aside and peered through the square single pane, spotting me over by the icebox. "Ivy May," he demanded, rattling the knob. "Unlock the door right now!" I moved to do his bidding. My mother covered her ears, but when he stepped into the kitchen, she suddenly dropped her hands and flew at him, beating his chest and screaming, "Marion's dead, isn't he? I know he's dead!" Then she moved away and said with an oddly calm voice, "I hate you for letting Birdie drive the tractor, and I hate God for letting Marion die!" She went into the bedroom and quietly closed the door. It was quiet in the house except for the half-hour chime of the dining room mantel clock.

Grandma Ada pulled my father to the table and put a cup of coffee in front of him. "She didn't mean it, Job. She's not thinkin' right just now." She stood behind him, massaging his neck gently until he reached up to still her hand.

"Don't, Ma. You and Pa go home. I think we need a little time to ourselves." Grandma Ada rinsed out the coffee cups, paused briefly at the closed bedroom door, thought the better of knocking, and followed my grandfather out the door. I was left alone with my father, more frightened than I had ever been in my life. He didn't stay in the kitchen long. "Best git to the chores, I suppose," he said, getting to his feet unsteadily.

That's the thing about farming city folks never seem to understand. No matter what happens, there are always chores—bushels of corn carried to the steers; bales of alfalfa thrown down, busted, and scattered for cud-chewing cows; pig waterers cleaned out; cows milked; and eggs picked. A farm grants no reprieve from chores, no time to grieve. In the midst of sorrow, the barn cats still line up in wait for their evening treat, a stream of warm milk squeezed from a teat and aimed in their direction.

The kitchen was a bleak place with its cold range and closed bedroom door. I decided I would put Grandma

Ada's goulash, tied up in a white dishtowel on the pantry counter, in the warming oven and ready the table for supper. I counted out five plates, knowing somehow that if my mother came out of the bedroom and saw Marion's place at the table empty, she would go back into her sanctuary and never come out. My father would have to take her to St. Peter, just like Dorie Ann's grandmother and Aunt Salome, and that would be the end of it. So I set out a plate for Marion along with his favorite glass, a saved Welch's jelly jar decorated with cartoon characters. Then I went to find Birdie.

The barn was quiet except for the sound of the cows moving their heads in the stanchions as they stretched to borrow hay from a neighbor. Standing around the corner of the feed room, I saw my father fill the hand sprayer, pump the handle, and mist the cows for flies before he grabbed his three-legged stool and pail and headed for the first cow. Suddenly, he slammed the pail against the cement wall of the barn and threw the stool into the gutter, splashing urine and manure. The barn erupted in a cacophony of racket as the cows pulled back in their stanchions and blatted in fright, the cats screeched and scattered, and my father leaned against the wall, head in hands, and sobbed, deep, wrenching sounds that came from a place I didn't know.

After a while, it was quiet. The cows settled down and the cats returned to their patient waiting. My father wiped his nose on the sleeve of his shirt and spoke in a quiet, tired voice that didn't much resemble my memory of his powerful delivery of "Invictus." "I know you're hidin' around the corner, Ivy May. Make yourself useful and bust a couple bales of alfalfa for the calves in the back pen. Then go find your brother."

I hesitated and then blurted out, "It wasn't Birdie's fault. Marion and me were throwin' . . ." The words stuck in my throat.

My father squirted a stream of milk at the cats and said, "I figured it was somethin' like that."

"Inez Benson said Birdie shouldn't have been drivin' the tractor. Birdie's gonna get blamed for something Marion and me did."

"Don't really care what that nosey old biddy thinks. There's enough blame to go around for all of us, and none of it changes a thing, Ivy May. Now do what I asked and git your brother."

It didn't take me long to find Birdie. He was curled up in the rope cranny, asleep, face sweaty and smudged from tears, his head cushioned in my mother's lap. Somehow, during the commotion in the milking parlor down below, she had left her bedroom, crept up the loft ladder, and found Birdie. In the movies, the mother always despairs, hating the child left behind, the one deemed less worthy . . . the one who should have died. Not so, my mother. She put her finger to her lips to shush and then gathered me to her side.

* * *

Unseasonably warm weather hung on through September that year, but our summer ended that day we lost Marion in a load of oats. It wasn't that life didn't go on. In Frost's blunt words, we weren't the ones dead, so we turned to our affairs. Dad fenced, cultivated the corn, and put up the second and third cuttings of alfalfa. Mom still pulled the Maytag into the kitchen to wash clothes on Monday, changed the bottom sheets on the beds every week, except for Marion's, pulled crabgrass out of her garden, and pruned her rose bushes. But there was no joy in any of it. The evening brought a pervasive darkness that had nothing to do with nightfall and everything to do with our loss. After supper, my mother hung her apron on its pantry peg and went into the bedroom, closing the door behind her and leaving an unspoken message: Quiet! Do Not Disturb! Dad took to spending the couple of hours before bedtime at the kitchen table, clearing his throat a lot as he read the *Wallace Farmer* or *Farm Journal* and sometimes worked in his farm management books.

For Birdie and me, it was as if our lives were on hold, like we awaited a signal that would put us into motion again. Even though nothing was said, I knew my piano lessons were over. My mother closed the old upright before we left for Marion's funeral, and it remained unopened. When Birdie finally got up enough nerve to take the uke down and tune it, my father looked up and said with uncharacteristic shortness, "Put it away, Birdie, or go outside with the damn thing." Then he added, "And quit smackin' your lips all the time. Where's that comin' from?"

Sometimes Birdie and I went outside to sit on the porch steps with Shep, but even the old dog huddled close to our knees and whined softly, sensing his family was falling apart.

"Wanna play tag, Birdie?" I asked one night, eager to break the silence.

He shook his head. "It's no fun without Marion." And then, "Does Marion know he's dead, Ivy May? Think he knows? What if he don't like it there?"

I covered my ears and wished I didn't feel so guilty for wanting to have a little fun.

The Chief End of Man

The Ames clan was Calvinist. Grandma Ada was proud to claim her father and grandfather were among the founding fathers of First Presbyterian. Grandpa Henry often bragged about his single-handedly building the church belfry, and, according to my father, complained for the rest of his life about the bozo who installed the bell and then skipped town during the night, leaving the Presbyterians with a bell that only tolled when it felt like it. In Munger, folks were pretty much either Presbyterian or Lutheran (the Missouri Synod variety); at least that's what they said, even though some hadn't darkened the door of the Lord's house since baptism. There were a few Catholics, too, but they had to worship in nearby Brewster or Worthington.

My friend Dorie Ann was Lutheran. I visited her church a time or two but didn't much care for the sing-song liturgy her poor minister had to chant every Sunday and for a good fifteen minutes of the service at that. He was embarrassingly off-key, flat as a pancake, even at the Gloria Patri, and he knew it, too, if his throat clearing and red ears were any indication. Dorothy Nelson, the church pianist, tried to help him find the pitch by frowning and loudly striking his note from time to time, but that only made things worse because it confused his flock. By the Benedictus, just a few weak voices labored on.

We Presbyterians were content with brief responsive readings and were able to languish in our pews while we read, unlike Dorie Ann and the Lutheran faithful who stood for most of the service—the liturgy, the Gospel reading, the Apostles' Creed, the Lord's Prayer, four stanzas each of at least four hymns, and the benediction. However, even though the Lutherans did a lot of standing, at least it prevented them from sticking to their pews in the summer like we did because the Ladies Aid had been too generous with Beacon Wax during their spring cleaning of the church. My father said Presbyterians were apt to rise up for the doxology and the closing hymn and depend on the preacher to take care of the rest of the worship and get it done in an hour. In my father's words, "If we don't get the gist of the sermon in twenty minutes, ten more ain't gonna save us!"

But when Dorie Ann invited me to her confirmation in September of our ninth-grade year, I went home envious. Confirmation was a big deal to the Lutherans. As Dorothy N. plunked out "All Hail the Power of Jesus' Name," the pastor led his charges in their long white robes up the center aisle to the front of the sanctuary, where his wife pinned a single red rose on each person in the class. Then they knelt at the rail to receive their first communion, and Dorie Ann said it was Mogen David, too, not the Welch's grape juice we had at First Presbyterian.

Dad said somewhere along the line, a little of the Methodists' teetotalism must have rubbed off on us, forcing Grandpa Moses to keep his half pint of Jim Beam, which he claimed was for medicinal purposes, hidden between the folds of the saddle blanket in the tack room. At the end of the service, Dorie Ann and her class paraded out to form a reception line where the parishioners shook their hands and relatives hugged and kissed them as if they had suddenly and miraculously been saved by the Light and were now on their way to Eternal Salvation. But that wasn't the half of it. Each family honored their anointed child with an open house—chicken salad, sloppy joes, and a decorated sheet cake from Hansen's Bakery in Worthington. Relatives and neighbors brought gifts. Besides the keepsake mustard-seed amulet from her parents, Dorie Ann raked in nearly fifty bucks.

Confirmation at First Presbyterian was a pretty plain affair. Admittedly, we fledging Calvinists didn't deserve anything quite so grand, for ours was a short course: only six weeks of studying the catechism and learning a little about church governance. While Dorie Ann studied with her pastor for two years, we met with Reverend Cox for six Sunday evenings and then lined up in front of the church to recite the catechism for the elders and the congregation.

My mother decided that Birdie and I would be confirmed together, much to my father's chagrin. "It's no use, Ruthie," he argued, "puttin' him through that nonsense. The good Lord doesn't give a tinker's damn about Birdie recitin' the catechism." Mother's calm response was that certainly God loved Birdie just the way he was, but—and it was a big but—the Heavenly Father also wanted him to keep trying to be the best he could be. "Well, Ruthie," Dad said, "I think God knows you can't make silk out of a sow's ear, but have it your way. You're hell-bent to try, and you always think you know what's best when it comes to Birdie." But his disgruntled tone voiced doubt of that. I think Reverend Cox wondered a bit, too, when the both of us showed up.

After two sessions, I was worried sick. I remembered the previous confirmation, when Bobby Olsen couldn't recite the answer to his question and the elders made him stand there and suffer through his memory loss, looking like a deer caught in the headlights, and then debated about his confirmation worthiness. How would Birdie ever memorize any of the catechism? It wouldn't work to make a crib sheet, because he couldn't read. For the thousandth time, I wished for Marion. He would have figured out a way to save Birdie.

I finally came up with a plan. The catechism was a small paperbound book with twenty-three questions that spoke to the tenets of Calvinist theology. "What is the chief end of man?" was the first question. It was the only question with a short answer, simply "The chief end of man is to glorify God and enjoy him forever." After that initial nugget of our faith, the questions became more complicated and the answers longer until, at the very end, the recitations were nearly a half page of small print. I thought with lots of practice Birdie could at least memorize the answer to the first question, so all I had to do was make sure he was the first person in the line that formed in the front of the church and thereby be asked the first question.

To be on the safe side, I would stand next to him as sort of a prompter. It was cheating, I knew, but I didn't think God would care if it helped Birdie find the Promised Land. Birdie and I worked on "What is the chief end of man?" every night for five weeks. "Am I very bright?" he asked repeatedly as we sat cross-legged on my bed and worked on the twelve-word answer. Granted, the deeply profound nature of it was beyond our young minds, but I did wonder why so many folks didn't get around to the second part of the response. They glorified, I supposed, by showing up for worship, but they didn't appear to enjoy it all that much. Otherwise, it seemed to me, they wouldn't be in such a hurry to get out of church every Sunday to claim a booth at Hannah's Café for coffee and apple pie before the Lutherans could get there.

The class, all six of us, was to be presented to the elders and congregation for examination at the end of the Maundy Thursday service. Mom drove to Worthington and bought Birdie a plaid sport jacket, white shirt, and fancy tie. I got a new dress at Andersons' Dress Shop, pink cotton piqúe with a scalloped neckline, and after some serious begging, a pair of black flats. Andersons' had a sweet deal. If you bought one dress for $8.95, you could get another for just a penny. They were last year's picked-over stock, but it was still a definite step up from feed sacks and my older cousin's hand-me-downs.

Birdie and I were ready an hour early. My father whistled his approval, tied a Windsor knot in Birdie's tie, took a picture of us with his old Kodak, and looked around for my mother. "Where's your mother?" he asked. The bedroom door was closed, and I knew that meant she was crying. I understood; she wanted Marion in the picture, too. My father pushed open the door and stood there. I could see her sitting on the side of the bed, staring at her reflection in the mirror. Dad sighed, "It won't bring him back, Ruthie. What's done is done." Then he added, "I know you keep all those horse pictures he drew under the bed and sneak a peek at 'em when nobody's lookin', but you gotta turn the page, woman. The kids and I need you." Then he closed the door and shooed us out to the car. We didn't have to wait very long before my mother, wearing her dignity like a fine cloak, slid into the front seat. My father reached over and squeezed her leg.

We were supposed to gather in the minister's study before the service. I had prayed mightily the night before. Usually, I just said "Now I lay me down to sleep," but I added a prayer that my plan would work and Birdie would be confirmed. God must have heard and gotten in touch with Reverend Cox, because he took one look at the bunch of us, winked at me, and said, "I think the fairest way to do this is to put you in alphabetical order, so Birdsel Ames, I guess you're number one, and Ivy May, you're next." I almost wet my pants I was so relieved. We filed into the church, but before the minister could even present us to the elders, Kenny Zapf had to open his big mouth. "Hey, Birdie, c'mon over here," he whispered, motioning with his arm. And like a lamb being led to slaughter and thrilled to be wanted by anybody, Birdie grinned and pulled away from my grasp on the sleeve of his sport coat. He went to the very end of the line and parked himself by Kenny.

Reverend Cox looked at me and shrugged. There was nothing he could do that wouldn't bring unwanted commotion to the serious occasion. "Ivy May Ames," he asked solemnly, "What is the chief end of man?" I wanted to grab Birdie and run down the aisle, past the front row where Grandma Ada and Grandpa Henry sat proud and tall, and my mother, leaning against my father, frantically wadded a damp handkerchief in her shaking hands, all the while wishing that Marion were not dead and buried under the scraggly evergreen in the cemetery south of town. Reverend Cox cleared his throat and repeated, "Ivy May?" and somehow the words rolled out.

Birdie's question was number six. The question itself was a half page. Reverend Cox looked uncomfortable, but forged ahead. "Birdsel, looks like the next question is yours." Birdie stood still as a statue and not a sound came out. The church was dead quiet. Not even the Jensen baby, who blatted like a sick calf every Sunday, made a peep. So Birdie and I did what we always did when the chips were down. First, I threw up. We'd had chili for supper, which didn't complement my pink pique dress, the burgundy carpet of the chancel, or Reverend Cox's new Nunn Bush wing tips.

THE CHIEF END OF MAN

And then Birdie covered his mouth and started to giggle. The minister shook his head at him, and Kenny gave him an elbow poke in the ribs, but there was no stopping the giggles, and that got Kenny and the rest of the class going. Suddenly, Reverend Cox had a divine revelation. He turned to the congregation with uplifted hands and with all the dignity he could muster under the circumstances, considering his vomit-splattered wing tips, spoke, "All in favor of receiving this class, signify by shouting amen." The church resounded with approval, the Jensen baby began to scream, and we skipped right to the last stanza of "Beneath the Cross of Jesus." The church cleared out fast, not a single handshake or hug. I escaped by the side door and ran to the car, my beautiful pink dress clinging to my legs in a sodden, sour mess.

It was a quiet ride home, except for Birdie's nonstop giggles. My mother didn't utter a word, but she didn't seem too upset. Maybe she was thinking there was more than one way to skin a cat. Dad looked over at her as we turned into our lane, shook his head, and asked, "You happy now, Ruthie?" I think Mom was.

Call to Serve

In the end, the human spirit devises its own way to survive. There is little choice to do otherwise. And so it was with my mother. First was denial, her steadfast refusal to accept the inevitable conclusion that no amount of time spent sounding out words, writing them five times each, and practicing them orally until bedtime would ever earn Birdie a gold star—in fact, not even a red star, the consolation symbol of improvement, no matter how small—on Friday's spelling test. Birdie had absolutely no long- or short-term memory when it came to reading and writing, and, unfortunately, those were the only skills worth measuring in Mrs. Markley's classroom.

It counted for naught that Birdie could change the oil in the John Deere, plow a straight furrow, or cultivate a field of corn without covering a single fledgling plant. So that September evening, when my mother threw up her hands and exclaimed, "It's no use. I give up! It's in one ear and out the other," was an epiphany of sorts, or a "God moment," as my Presbyterian pastor liked to call it, and the end of a personal journey leading her from denial to hurt, to anger, and finally to quiet disappointment. In tears, she crumpled up Birdie's spelling list, lifted the front lid on the cookstove, and set it afire . . . along with her hope that if she really put her mind to it, Birdie could learn, wake up smart like Marion, and all would be well in the Ames family. It was not to be, and my mother knew it.

When Birdie first started missing a day of school here and there to help my father around the farm, I felt guilty relief. For a few hours, I didn't have to worry about keeping an eye on him. The kids, big and small, never tired of their sport. They loved to get him going and then laugh at his silliness. "Stop it, Bird!" I'd yell as he chased them around the schoolyard to reclaim his cap or lunch bucket.

"We're just having fun, Ivy May," he'd say, his face red with exertion.

I wanted to grab him and scream, "Can't you see they're making fun of you?" But Birdie never did. And with Marion gone, there was no one to fight his battles. I was a feeble defender, mostly holding back tears and praying for recess to be over and that my father might need Birdie to help around the farm the next day. I had learned my lesson in fourth grade, when I ran to get Miss B. because two eighth-grade boys had Birdie pinned to the ground and were making him eat grass, but she was busy gossiping with another teacher and didn't much like my interruption. "Ivy May," she said reprovingly, "what have I said about tattling?" Then she added, "Birdsel needs to take care of his own problems, and you need to mind your own business. Shoo now." As I turned away, I heard her add, "My word, I declare I don't understand why they don't take that poor dummy out of school. What's the point, really?"

When Birdie was in the eighth grade, Superintendent Shanker took my father aside and asked him if he were aware that, according to state law, Birdie could drop out of school at the end of eighth grade or when he turned sixteen. He mentioned as well that some parents were a little uncomfortable with Birdie being in the same classroom with their younger children, so, all things considered, it might be best for Birdie to try his hand at something else. The suggestion was a hurtful, bitter pill for my mother to swallow. There were the usual tears. "I hate to give up the ship, Job," she told my father. "It's like saying we don't care what happens to Birdie."

"Guess I see it the other way, Ruthie," my father said. "To my way of thinkin', this ship you're talkin' about has been takin' in water for quite a spell. Maybe it's time to find another boat." Birdie was sixteen a week later, and my mother sent a note with me that same day to let the teacher know Birdie was done with school. Birdie didn't seem a bit sad, just relieved and glad his coloring days were finally over. He donned his bibs and yellow DeKalb cap and became a full-time farmer.

* * *

In '51, the Korean War was mired down in frigid, sucking mud. The headlines were big and dire as hordes of Red soldiers crossed the border into North Korea. General Douglas MacArthur urged the president to order American troops to push them back into China, and, in an ill-advised decision that backfired, went public when his commander-in-chief refused. A feisty Truman fired his outspoken five-star general, much to the chagrin of many Americans, including my parents. My father shook his head, and my mother wept as she listened over the Philco to MacArthur's sad farewell speech to Congress. "Old soldiers never die," he said. "They just fade away." But my cousin Jake offered a different take on the general's fall from grace. He was in the Philippines during World War II when MacArthur made good on his promise to return. Jake said the old man, corncob pipe in hand, waded ashore after the danger of sniper fire was over, like he was a goddam king, a real asshole, in his estimation anyway. My mother didn't buy it, though. Nobody could persuade her General Douglas MacArthur wasn't the real McCoy, a true-blue American soldier.

But Ruthie Ames wasn't so enamored with the military when her son got his notice from the local Selective Service Board. Birdie was to present himself at the Hotel Thompson in Worthington on the twenty-third day of June for the purpose of draft classification. The bus would leave at eight thirty in the morning for Sioux Falls, South Dakota, and return in late afternoon after mental and physical exams. As our neighbor Emil often put it, the shit hit the fan when my mother opened that letter. She ran all the way up the lane from the mailbox and straight down to the pig barn where my father, Birdie, and I were sorting the spring barrows and gilts, waved the letter across the partition, and yelled, "He can't do it, Job! You've got to call someone."

Over the snuffling grunts of the agitated pigs, my father yelled back, "What the hell you talkin' about, Ruthie? I can't hear a damn thing you're sayin'." Sorting done, my father hopped over the fence, took the letter my mother pushed at him, read it, and handed it back with a shrug. "Not much we can do about it, Ruthie. Birdie is what he is, and it's probably best they see it for themselves."

"But he can't, Job! He won't know where to go or what to do. He'll get lost. Sioux Falls isn't Munger, you know. Someone could knock him over the head and . . ." Her voice trailed off in tears.

"Oh, for God's sake, settle down, woman! That ain't likely, and you know it. Stop your worryin' and put the coffee pot on. Any of that apple pie left?" Then he added, "If it'll make you feel any better, I'll talk to the recruitin' officer when I put Birdie on the bus."

My mother turned away, but not without a parting shot. "What if Birdie gets sent to Korea, Job? He doesn't even know how to fire a gun."

Laughing, my father said, "Careful, Ruthie, you're gettin' way ahead of yourself. Besides, that's what they aim to teach 'em in the army."

* * *

On the fateful day Birdie was to board the bus for Sioux Falls, my father decided that, since we were making the trip to Worthington anyway, he might as well kill two birds with one stone. A couple of days before, he had weaned a little Holstein heifer from its mother. We didn't feed out dairy stock, so the two or three calves we had annually were sent to the Livestock Sales Barn to be sold as veal. Like most of our farm neighbors, we butchered our own meat, a corn-fed steer and a barrow or two every year, as well as thirty or forty spring fryers, and my father figured a veal cutlet once in a while would taste good, too.

But my mother would have none of it. "Well, you'll have to fix it yourself then, Job. I'm not. It turns my stomach to even think of eating a little thing like that." I totally sided with my mother's opinion. Had I been born a few decades later, I'm sure I would have ended up a vegan. Home butchering was not for the faint of heart. Using a rope and pulley from the haymow, my father hoisted an animal up by the hind feet, slit its throat to bleed it out—saving a pail for Grandma Ada, who liked to make blood sausage—and then sent me to the house with another pail holding the tongue and heart for my mother to pickle. Grandpa Henry said it was a real treat to finish off a nice slice of either one on a saltine cracker. Talk about disgusting!

For a smart man, my father came up with some oddball ideas from time to time. This one was a corker. He took the back seat out of the Ford, laid down a square of tarp, and prepared to load the little heifer. My mother had been watching from the pantry window, and when he tried to lift the scared, balky animal into the car, she flew out of the house, whaling her house broom at anything within reach, including my father's backside. "Job Ames, have you completely lost your mind?"

Hanging on to the terrified heifer with one arm and using the other to ward off my mother's wicked broom, my father settled the argument quickly when he said, "Well, it's either a trip to the sales barn or veal cutlets for supper. It's your call, Ruthie." My mother backed off, but not before she sailed her broom into the dooryard to land in an inconvenient mud puddle. "I guess we're just a bunch of hillbillies after all," she bit out. "Now Birdie will smell like manure. That's bound to really impress the recruiter." The porch screen door nearly fell off its hinges as she slammed her way back into the house.

My father turned to me, "Ivy May, give me hand here. Hop in the car and hold onto 'er head after I lift 'er in." The unthinkable dawned on me in that instant. My father's transportation plan directly involved his fourteen-year-old daughter, a pathetic creature already struggling with puberty and self-esteem issues. He actually expected me to ride in the back with the frantic little calf, which was already spewing urine and poop like there was no tomorrow. Even Birdie, all dressed up in new blue jeans for the bus ride to Sioux Falls, was dumbstruck.

"I'll do it, Ivy May," he said and started toward the car.

But my father was adamant that I be the goat that day. He said Birdie couldn't risk getting poop on his new jeans, and it wouldn't hurt me any. "A little shit or veal cutlets, Ivy May." Had I been a God-fearing Catholic instead of a Presbyterian, I would have been working my beads mightily. As it were, I just offered a prayer that no one I knew would see me, and that my father would somehow suffer for the outrageous indignity he was imposing on me. He did his usual thing: drove slower than anybody else on the road and hummed and whistled all the way to town. Every car that passed us slowed down and nearly drove off the road before leaving us in a cloud of dust. Birdie tried not to giggle, and I vowed to run away from home the next day.

We dropped the heifer off and then drove to the Hotel Thompson to meet Birdie's bus. My father had not been truthful with my mother. He didn't say a word to the recruiter who checked Birdie off the list and told him to get on the bus.

Mom spent the afternoon scolding my father under her breath and scrubbing the inside of the Ford. The three of us met the bus at four o'clock. There was a big sigh of relief when Birdie was the first one off. He must have fared just fine because, as the rest of guys got off the bus, each one clapped Birdie on the back and told him to take care of himself and get that cultivating done. We didn't have to wonder what Birdie talked about on the bus ride over and back to Sioux Falls.

Birdie got his Selective Service classification about a month later 4-F. When Dad read the notice for him, he asked, puzzled, "How come I got F? The guys on the bus said I did real good."

Diversity

Sociologists would probably never describe rural communities as diverse—that is, if they were much interested in describing them at all. Their statistics usually get stuck in graphing the big picture, the all-consuming conversation about the racial and economic divide of the urban landscape. They forget about the unique makeup of the small town, considered just a wide spot in the road by most city folk, a place where a bunch of retired farmers hang out in the back room of the pool hall and play a few hands of pinochle while they complain about the price of corn and wait for their wives to finish serving the funeral luncheon for Mrs. Psysk down at First Presbyterian.

But, in fact, diversity thrives in the small town. It's definitely not one of those gated communities that aims to exclude the kind of folks who might consider dragging their used sofa down to the street and plunking a "Free" sign on it—unless, of course, you want to count the fancy grill-iron fence out at the cemetery south of town that doesn't even keep out the known sinners. In a small town, there's no yuppie, white-collar neighborhood where everyone is under fifty and all vehicles, including RVs, must be parked in the garage, and where's there's not a chance in hell you'd ever visit across the fence with a farm widow who works her egg shells and morning coffee grounds into the soil around her flourishing rose bushes.

The makeup of my childhood hometown, Munger, was eclectic, to say the least. A neighbor probably still had an outdoor privy and kept a few old laying hens in a small coop in the backyard, because fresh eggs, especially the little brown ones, were so much better than store-bought. And West of Main Street, John Ulfers, not yet ready to give up the plow but coaxed into moving to town by Ella because it was high time to get off the home place and leave the chores to their son and his new wife, usually parked his John Deere alongside the house, ready for his daily trip to the farm.

Next door, Mrs. Kotke kept to herself and, despite her crippling arthritis, still lovingly cared for her severely retarded adult son, somehow managing with a strange belt contraption to drag him out to the front porch every day for a little fresh air. And just a block over, a transplant from the East Coast—New York City, for heaven's sake— kept her shades pulled around the clock, but shared her artistic talents with the community by designing sets for the high school's three-act play and reading O. Henry's "Gift of the Magi" without a microphone to a packed town hall on Santa Claus Day. And, of course, there was my brother Birdie, chocolate double-dipper in hand, usually off at a trot somewhere and grinning all the while.

I guess the variety was good, and it did seem, growing up, as if everyone had a niche. Town kids had their own spot in the scheme of things. They went roller skating, had hamburgers at Hannah's or Eddie's Pool Hall, and bought Cokes at the gas station. And farm kids, like Dorie Ann, Birdie, and me, played our part, too. We were in 4-H and showed black Angus or Herefords at the county fair, ate our big meal at noon, and found enjoyment in a cool glass of Watkins orangeade made with rusty well water. I used to think social status depended on whether your family had running water in the house, along with an indoor john, but when my father finally made a bathroom out of the pantry, it didn't seem to change things much. Birdie and I were still farm kids.

But most of the time, nobody much noticed or cared, the general thought being "It is what it is" . . . unless, of course, somebody overstepped a boundary, self-imposed or not, like if Mrs. Kotke had suddenly shown up out of the blue to lend a hand in making the vegetable barley beef soup for the fall church bazaar. It wouldn't have caused a hole in the universe, but there would have been some raised eyebrows, more rubbering than usual on the party lines around town, and, of course, the question, spoken or unspoken, "Whatever was Mrs. Kotke thinking?" Obviously, she didn't know that it was Helen Peterson's secret recipe, and Helen handpicked her own helpers to brown the meat and chop the vegetables, and only she added just the right pinch of allspice to "warm" the broth.

And Birdie had his niche, too. He had to remember to "stay in the lines." Sometimes he forgot . . . forgot that he should be ashamed to be so foolish . . . to be so friendly . . . to be so happy about nothing . . .

* * *

Had it been up to my mother, I would never have dated. According to her, boys were after one thing, and it wasn't just a kiss goodnight at the door of our farmhouse. So when Lenny Peterson finally got up enough gumption to ask if I wanted to go to the Doris Day movie at the State Theater in Worthington on Sunday night, she frowned and tightly pursed her lips, which meant a big no was about to come my way. "Ivy May," she said, brooking no argument, "there's school the next day, and I don't think your father would approve."

Pretty sure my father wouldn't give a darn one way or the other, I headed for the barn to ask him. He was singing "Amazing Grace" while he forked some fresh manure out of the gutter. It seemed to me if he felt the need to sing a hymn, he could have chosen several more fitting, but then Dad always said it would be a good thing if everybody had to pitch a little manure from time to time. To his way of thinking, it made a fellow humble . . . and that's a big part of grace . . . and sure as hell helped him get a handle on where the bacon and steak came from. I stayed by the door, thinking that if I did get to go out with Lenny, I didn't want my hair to smell like cow poop.

Our only soft water came from a cistern by the house, which caught the summer rain off the roof and, unfortunately, also captured the spotted salamanders we tossed out in the annual spring cleaning, along with a garden snake or two. In the winter we had to buy water, so nightly sponge baths and weekly hair washings were the extent of our cleanliness. Years later, my daughter Maren let me know how it grossed her out to even hear me talk about the good old days. "My God, Mother," she complained, "give it a rest. You make it sound like you grew up in a third-world country!"

"Dad," I asked, "is it all right if I go with Lenny Peterson to see the Doris Day movie Sunday night?"

My father stopped in midpitch and laughed. "Lenny? That little guy's a head shorter than you, Ivy May. I'll have to put a milk stool out by the back step for him to stand on if he's thinkin' about a goodnight kiss." He heaved his steaming forkful out the door, where Birdie waited with the manure spreader and moved down the gutter.

"Dad, he's a senior!"

"Don't cut no cake, Ivy May. He's still short. What happened to tall, dark, and handsome?"

I almost blurted out that tall, dark, and handsome guys don't date girls with names like Ivy May, especially if they have goofy brothers. Dorie Ann told me that Butch Hines, who was new in school and really good-looking, was thinking about asking me out, but when she told him who I was, he rolled his eyes and said, "No shit? Not a chance I'd be askin' her out. Her brother's a moron . . . always laughin' about nothin'." I felt the usual clutch in my heart that was always there when somebody picked on Birdie, and I was mad at Dorie Ann for telling me what Butch said. I felt like reminding her that not even the short boys asked her out, and she didn't have any brother, goofy or not, to scare them away.

Even though Dorie Ann was my best friend, she said mean things sometimes, like when she told me our family wasn't invited to the monthly neighborhood card parties because of Birdie. "Who cares?" I shot back, "My folks think playing cards is a big waste of time anyway." I would never let Dorie Ann know it, but it was hurtful. What had Birdie ever done to any of them? He was good enough to help them when they needed an extra hand to pitch manure.

My father leaned on the handle of his fork for a moment while he honked his nose into the straw and then said, "Up to your ma, I guess. That's her department." He threw another dripping load out the barn door and hollered for Birdie to spread it on the oat stubble south of the pig barn.

I meandered back to the house, wondering how I could soften my mother's resistance. She was at the kitchen table, rolling out piecrust, unusual because that was always a Saturday chore and it was only Wednesday. "Apple or cherry?" I asked, wondering if maybe she had an ulterior motive to her midweek pie baking. She'd been dropping hints about getting a new range . . . especially if it had one of those new deep wells and a broiler under the oven. My mother knew how to play her cards from time to time, too. A warm piece of cherry pie to go along with my father's afternoon coffee wasn't a bad idea at all.

"Cherry, I guess. It's your dad's favorite."

Something was definitely cooking. "Are we having company?" I asked, already knowing the answer. She carefully laid the pastry over the pie plate, took the thickened filling off the stove, spread it over the bottom crust and then deftly rolled, fitted, and trimmed the top crust. With a little brushed-on egg white for a nice golden brown, a few sprinkles of sugar, and some pokes with a table fork to vent the air, her masterpiece was finished.

"No," she said, "just thought your father might be getting a little tired of cookies and cake."

I knew better, and that knowledge gave me a sudden inspiration. "Mom," I said, "you should get Dad to buy you a new range. Dorie Ann's mother got a Deluxe Hotpoint and she just loves it."

My mother slid the pie into the oven, propped the kitchen broom against the door to hold it shut, and turned to face me. "Well, Ivy May, you and I both know Dorie Ann's father isn't one to hang on to his money like your father. My word, that Lizzie gets a new davenport every other year, and I just make do with what I got. Of course, it's a different story with your father when it comes to buying something for the farm, like that newfangled side rake he had no business coming home with. A few minutes looking around in Ling's Implement seems to loosen the purse strings in a hurry."

"You should just tell Dad you want a new range."

"I shouldn't have to tell him, Ivy May. He's got eyes, hasn't he? Does he think I prop the broom against the oven door just for the fun of it?" My mother didn't often

share her feelings with me, so I felt a sudden closeness at
her venting.

* * *

At supper that night, as I was passing the fried potatoes
and sausage to Birdie, I said, "Dad, you should get Mom one
of those new Deluxe Hotpoint ranges. Then she wouldn't
have to prop the oven door shut with the broom."

"Hasn't said nothin' to me about wantin' a new stove,
Ivy May." He reached across to take the plate from Birdie.
"The checkbook's over in the drawer, Ruthie. Your name's
on it, too."

My mother's face suddenly looked a little flushed. "Well,"
she said, "it would be nice to have a little better range now
that the threshers are about due. Maybe Ivy May and I'll drive
into Worthington and see what Rickbeils have on sale."

"Oh, Mom," I ventured, thinking my timing couldn't be
better, "I asked Dad about going to the Doris Day movie
with Lenny Peterson, and he said it was up to you." But
it was as if she had already forgotten that I had laid the
groundwork for her new range.

"Ivy May, we've already discussed this."

Then Birdie saved the day, "I like Lenny. He's nice to
me. He said he'd buy me a double-dipper next time he saw
me in town. We gonna have ice cream for dessert?"

My mother's face instantly softened. "Well, I suppose it
wouldn't hurt, if you're home right after the movie." Then
she reached over to pat Birdie's arm and added, "Lenny
does seem to be a nice young man."

It wouldn't be the last time Birdie came to my rescue. I could hardly wait to ask Dorie Ann if she'd noticed that Butch Hines had ears the size of saucers, and they were so dirty you could plant potatoes in them.

Rebirth

The feminist movement was still a decade away when I graduated from Munger High in '55. Betty Friedan had yet to give voice to dissatisfied housewives and mothers across the land aching for a sense of inner fulfillment beyond the walls of home-sweet-home with her book *The Feminine Mystique*. For sure, nobody was burning bras in Munger, and girdles—even a few corsets—were still moving in JC Penney's lingerie department.

Personally, I was completely dumb about what a woman could do if she put her mind to it. In my corner of the world, for God's sake, women still ate last at family gatherings, whatever was left after the men folk dished up ample portions and sometimes even second helpings for themselves. The women I knew were mostly farm wives who not only reared their several children, but also kept a tidy house and huge garden, and could pitch a load of manure and help put up the hay if need be. The few spinsters who escaped this exciting rural life of service to husbands and children ventured into teaching or nursing, or became the talk of the town when they lit out for Minneapolis and a job in retail sales at Dayton's. But fortunately for me, my mother had a two-year teaching degree, and she encouraged me to think outside the box, or in my case, the farmyard.

A career in nursing sounded glamorous. I was especially drawn to the white starched uniforms and perky
caps that nurses wore. Sadly, that classy attire eventu-
ally gave way to baggy, drawstring pajamas and flowered
smocks, and now it's hard to tell a nurse from the custo-
dian mopping up the floor. Who knows? Maybe I was
unknowingly saved from future disappointment. But the
truth was, I struggled with even ninth-grade algebra, and
my precollege inventory emphasized that I should stay far
afield from any career that suggested a need for compe-
tence in math and science. That pretty much eliminated
nursing and left marriage and teaching as career options.

But alas, short Lenny Peterson stayed short and fell in
love with my best friend, Dorie Ann, of all people, and left
St. Mary's Catholic Church to become a dedicated Missouri
Synod Lutheran in hopes of persuading her folks he was
the right kind of fellow for their daughter. Dorie Ann
asked me to be her maid of honor after I convinced her
that Lenny and I hadn't made out in the back seat of his
green Ford the night he took me to the Doris Day movie at
the State Theater. It was a huge, fancy June wedding, on
account of both families being related to everyone else in
the county and also because the previous year had yielded
a bumper crop of corn, and Dorie Ann's folks could spare
the cash for a big splash. There was a sit-down chicken
dinner in the church basement after the ceremony, and
then we polkaed the night away at the town hall to the
music of Eddie Skeets. I had to admit Lenny and Dorie
Ann made a fine couple as they paraded down the aisle

after the ceremony, both short . . . and dreamy-eyed about their future on the Peterson farm east of town.

I spent the summer typing and measuring aerial maps for the local ASC office and didn't have a single date. Well, the best man from Dorie Ann's wedding did call me once, but he was even shorter than Lenny. I was beginning to wonder what there was about me that so attracted short men.

Mom said she thought I would do all right as a teacher, and Mankato was as good a place as any to go, so come September, she and Dad drove me north to Mankato State Teachers College, dumped me and my two pieces of aqua Samsonite luggage by the back door of Daniel Buck Hall, and headed home, saying they'd see me at Thanksgiving.

I didn't know it then, because I was petrified at the thought of leaving Munger and my big-toad-in-a-little-puddle status, but it was the beginning of my rebirth. When the freshman who slouched next to me in English Composition 101 leaned over and jabbed his pencil at my name, which was printed neatly in the upper the corner of my spiral notebook, and laughingly shook his head while whispering, "Ivy May?" followed by, "You gotta be right off the farm," I thought I was in the same old pickle, labeled a hick because of my backwoods name. The fact that I was wearing red anklets to match my red blouse probably had a little something to do with his quick assessment, too.

But about two weeks into Professor Maakestad's class, the Edina flash realized that, despite my being a countrified lass with a drippy name, I could write a pretty good essay, something he apparently hadn't learned in his big-city school, and Big Shot went from condescending to supplicating. Overnight, I became Ames or Iv, not only to the boy from a ritzy suburb, but also to a few of his friends who needed to pass English Comp 101 to keep their spots on the Indians' football squad.

I traded my colored anklets for roll-down bobby socks, bought a few cable-knit sweaters at Brett's Department Store, and invested in a pair of white tennis shoes, which I immediately rubbed with cigarette ash to make them look old and dirty. And in moment of utter abandonment, I even bought a pack of Cools and tried blowing smoke rings in the dorm smoker lounge. Ivy May Ames was a new woman in a new age.

I never talked about Birdie, at least not until I met Bill, except to say I had an older brother who helped my dad on the farm. Thinking back to the day I left home, I often wondered if Birdie had a sense then that things would never be quite the same again, at least not for a long time. "You're comin' back, aren't yuh, Ivy May?" was his worried question. He stood at the end of the lane, waving until he was just a small figure in the distance. He pretty much stayed there for the next thirty years, just a blip on my radar screen, and I didn't feel all that unhappy about it. I was off the farm, out of Munger, away from weekly visits to Marion's grave, and always . . . always . . . conveniently busy with my work and family.

* * *

Nothing seemed to change much until a warm Wednesday afternoon in September of '78. I was about to put a double lasagna in the oven for Maren's cross-country team's potluck when the phone rang. It was Dorie Ann, of all people. Our friendship had dwindled to a yearly exchange of Christmas greetings, in her case a lengthy letter detailing the successes of her children and describing their darling offspring. Dorie Ann didn't waste words that day. "Sorry to hear about your dad, Ivy May. Just wanted you to know Lenny and I are thinking of you and your mom." I could find no words. "Ivy May," she said. "Are you there?" Then after a long pause, "Oh, my God, Ivy May, you don't know. I shouldn't have called." Then she babbled something about it being such a sad day for our family and that Lenny would soon be in for supper, so she'd best go. I left the lasagna on the counter with a note for Bill and the kids and headed for Munger.

My mother and Birdie were waiting for me in the living room, sitting on either end of the old, plastic-covered couch. Mom had a vacant look about her, and Birdie was picking his bloody thumbnail and smacking his lips so frantically that he'd created white froth at the corners of his mouth. "Hi, Bird," I said softly, stilling his hand and holding him close. Everything's going to be fine." Then I knelt down in front of my mother, "Oh, Mom, what happened to Dad?"

She shrugged as if not understanding it herself. "I was at church for Ladies Aid. It's the third Wednesday of the month, you know. I stayed a bit longer than usual to help Elsie finish up the dishes. Kind of hard for her with her arthritis and all." Then she stopped and looked over at Birdie. "Stop picking that thumbnail, Birdie. You're going to get a bad infection if you keep doing that. How many times do I have to tell you not to do that?"

"Birdie's okay, Mom. Just tell me what happened."

"I stopped at the butcher shop for some of that good summer sausage your dad likes and then came right home. I probably should have stopped at the Mel's for your father's blood pressure pills. I think he's about out."

"Mom, please . . ."

"It seemed odd that Cato was waiting by the steps. That old dog never leaves your father's side except to chase the cats. Birdie was in the house . . . having a cookie, I guess. I told him to take the tractor out to the field where your dad was plowing under the alfalfa and see if he was having trouble or needed help. That's where Birdie found your dad, Ivy May, lying in the field. The coroner said he'd probably been dead most of the afternoon . . ." Then the tears started to flow. "And there I was at the church . . . the whole time . . . having dessert and coffee . . . while your father lay out there in the hot sun . . ." Birdie stopped picking and started to wail.

* * *

The good folks of Munger gathered to comfort in the way they knew best. Emil stepped in to help with the farm chores. Kind friends and the Presbyterian ladies filled the refrigerator with enough Jell-O salads and tuna hot dishes to feed most of Munger. Helpful farm neighbors managed the harvest. And then, once again, those who were not the one dead went on with their affairs. My mother did what she had to do. She made plans to sell the farm and move into town. It was a necessary decision, but not an easy one. And then getting ready for the farm auction was an arduous task. There were forty years of nails, bolts, screws, grease guns, fly sprayers, ropes, cattle and hog feeders, you name it—somewhere in the machine shed—to be sorted into boxes. In a way, the huge chore was good because it kept Mom and Birdie busy. Emil took charge, and Bill and I came down a couple of weekends to lend a hand. Our two kids, after some significant eye rolling, even came along to help.

I didn't sense that Birdie really understood that his niche was gone until he saw his beloved John Deere, purchased by a neighbor after some competitive bidding, being driven out of the farmyard. There were really no words to describe his stricken face, except to say he had the same lost look that fateful day we buried Marion.

Smart in the Heart

It was my weekend to spend with Birdie, and I faced the prospect with a pervading sense of reluctance and guilty obligation. The drive down was interminably long, almost two hundred miles across countryside I had seen countless times before, drab and lonely in its early November landscape of stubbled cornfields and black furrows. I was tired and cranky after a busy week of teaching, irritable at the thought of the five sections of personal narratives needing margin suggestions and grades before the coming Monday. Bill had decided to stay home; too many fall chores to do, according to him. I so wanted to say, "Lucky you, Bill," but instead I bit out, "Like what?"

"Well, I probably should restack the wood pile, Iv. Suppose they'll be here with that half cord one of these weekends."

I didn't buy that lame excuse. "They said towards the end of November, Bill, not the first." Then I added crossly, "Oh, forget it!" After a perfunctory peck on my cheek, he closed the car door, lit his pipe, and stood aside as I backed down the driveway, going off the edge of the tar as usual, which invariably caused him to holler impatiently, "Use your rearview mirror, Iv. There's a reason for its bein' there." And surely enough, as I turned to give a final wave, Bill was mouthing those very words, proving once again there aren't many surprises after forty years of togetherness.

My mother and I hadn't ever really discussed what would happen to Birdie when she died. I suppose a psychologist would call that a classic example of passive avoidance behavior in the both of us. My preference was that she had eternal life here on Earth, of course, but that was my idea, not my mother's. Despite her fierce love for Birdie, after more than a half century of caretaking, she was ready to join the heavenly throng and the leave the job to someone else. I knew the question of Birdie's future had always frightened her. She'd rather someone else made the difficult decisions. I had my fingers crossed that I would be excluded, too. Really, how could anyone possibly look forward to making plans for someone else to live life alone, especially if it were a person like Birdie? In our last telephone conversation, Mom said, "I've saved a little for Birdie over the years and there's the house. Do what you think is best, Ivy May." Not much direction.

After the funeral, Birdie had come home with Bill and me, but after a few days, he was restless, following me around the house and telling me over and over how he'd called 911 when he found Mom on the living-room floor but didn't touch anything because he didn't want to get into trouble. "Was I being bright when I called 911? I didn't touch nothin' because I didn't want 'em to think I did it."

"You did great, Birdie, just great," I assured him.

"I didn't touch nothin', Ivy May. Was I bein' bright not to do that?" And on and on . . .

To pass the time, Birdie and I made several trips to the DQ for chocolate double-dippers, and Bill and I took him roller skating. But even with the both of us on either side to hold him upright, the outing ended in a cracked wrist and tears, Birdie's and mine. I had forgotten he was an eight year old in a fifty-eight-year-old body. While we waited in the emergency room at the hospital, Bill informed me it was a pretty stupid idea to begin with. Just asking for trouble was how he put it. "Oh," I said, miffed at his convenient hindsight, "and I suppose you have all the answers. I only wanted him to have a little fun for a change, Bill. Is that so bad?"

"You're just feeling guilty, Iv, because you think Bird never had a chance to do the things you did. How do you know he even wanted to? Seems to me Bird's idea of fun has been driving the tractor, doing any odd job that comes his way, playing the spoons when he can get somebody to watch and listen, sitting down to a good meal of chicken, mashed potatoes, and corn, and topping it off with a double-dipper. He's a simple fellow, Iv. Don't try to make life complicated for him." Then Bill added, "You're always looking for the rainbow, Iv, but I think Birdie's the smart one. He's pretty much learned to dance in the rain."

"And when did you get to be such a wonderful philosopher, Bill Hansen? Oh, it's just that I don't know what to do, Bill."

"Try talking to him, Iv. He might have a few ideas of his own." Then Bill lifted his hand, palm facing outward as if to ward off any responsibility, and added, "I just know I'm staying out of it . . . not my business." I couldn't fault Bill. When I finally decided my senior year of college that it was time to take him home to meet my family, he wasn't scared off like Butch Hines (who, incidentally and much to my unrequited joy, aged into a fat slug with a giant beer belly). Instead, Bill sat right down with Birdie, talked tractors and mowers, chorded on the piano while he played the spoons, and even took him into town for a double-dipper. As we headed back to school, he pulled me close and said, "Bird's a good guy, Iv. You should be proud of him." I already thought I loved Bill, but that sealed the deal for me.

Thinking it over, I decided Bill's advice was on the mark, so the next afternoon, I asked Birdie if he wanted to go to the DQ for a chocolate double-dipper. He grinned, reached for his DeKalb cap, and said, "I'll treat," and then, predictably, as we got in the car, "Better put on your seat belt, Ivy May. You don't wanna go through the windshield and cut your head off like Bud Larson. Do you think there was a lot of blood, Ivy May? I bet there was."

Oh, God, I thought, how many more times would I have to hear that sad tale? A few years later, a psychologist who thought she had all the answers said Birdie was exhibiting perseveration when he persisted in saying the same thing over and over again, and we should think about some behavior-management strategy, you know, rewards and punishments. Oh, swell, and what would those be? Time outs? Single helpings of vegetables? Pretty hard, I thought to take something away from someone who hasn't much to begin with.

Double-dippers in hand, Birdie and I sat down at a shaded picnic table near the DQ. He happily licked his cone, ignoring the napkin I handed him, and asked, "Did Marion like double-dippers, too, Ivy May?"

"Oh, for heaven's sake, Birdie," I answered impatiently, "Marion's been gone almost fifty years. It doesn't matter."

"Marion never spilled. Remember how he could slick his cone, Ivy May?" And then, Birdie added, "I'm not very bright, am I?"

"Why? Because you spill? So do I," I said, laughing and pointing to the blob of ice cream on the front of my blouse. Lately it had become a common occurrence, causing my son to tease that old ladies must like to wear their food on their boobs.

"Is it dark there?"

"Where, Birdie?" I questioned, not following his thoughts.

"After you die. Is it dark where Marion is?"

Birdie looked worried. He had never liked the dark. I reached my hand across the table to cover his and said, "Birdie, do you remember what it was like before you got here?" He shook his head. I continued, "Maybe it will be like that when we die. We won't know."

Birdie grinned. "Boy!" he said, taking a big mouthful of ice cream and leaving a sizable chocolate mustache on his upper lip, "People are sure gonna be surprised when they get there and find out they're just dead. They're gonna be awful surprised, Ivy May." Birdie often said what a lot of people think but are afraid to voice, especially the soft-shelled agnostics Pastor Jef describes who sort of "walk the walk," just in case.

My brother had no such filters, another example of his not staying in the lines, I suppose. A well-meaning Bible thumper once told me smugly that it must be hard for a poor old guy like Birdie to understand the concept of heaven and eternal life. I could hardly refrain from responding that Birdie wasn't the only one around who struggled to make sense of the hereafter, but I had learned early on that there was a double standard for Birdie. If he repeated a racy story he'd heard down at the café, he was perverted, but the other fellow, well, he was rewarded with chuckles, knee slapping, and "That's a good one, Joe."

One time, when Birdie was driving his old Allis-Chalmers home after helping a neighbor pitch manure, he stopped to help a woman who was stranded along side the road with flat tire on her old jalopy. Birdie wouldn't think of doing anything else but lending a hand. He found the jack and spare in the trunk and told her to sit in the car with the three kids. He'd have it fixed in no time. Afterwards, she didn't even offer a thank-you before she drove off. Birdie didn't care. He said she probably was in a hurry to get home.

The next day, though, the sheriff drove out from Worthington to talk to my mother and ticket Birdie. It seemed the Good Samaritan was at fault for using his tractor for transportation, but mostly, I suspect, because the woman had reported that a retarded man had stopped to help her. Yikes! Heaven forbid! Interestingly, no one thought to alert the authorities that the retired farmer down the street was driving his tractor out to the home place every day because he was, you know, "all there." My mother got her dander up over that one. She backed the '67 Fury out of the garage and drove to Worthington to hire a lawyer. In the end, she paid the fifty-dollar fine and sold Birdie's tractor the next day . . . but not before she said her piece.

Ah, yes, the double standard. In truth, if Birdie had dished out just some of the rude and even obscene remarks that others daily sent his way, there would have been whispers . . . "Maybe a nice group home . . . in another community."

* * *

Remembering the reason for our little trip to the Dairy Queen, I pressed on. "Birdie, we have to decide some things."

"What things?"

"Well, like where you should live now that Mom's gone. Things like that."

He stopped in midlick, his eyes wide with surprise. "I got my job, Ivy May." Birdie had a Green Thumb job with the city. He mowed the cemetery and park, emptied garbage, helped with snow removal, and loved every minute of it. It put change in his pocket and made him feel important, like he was a regular guy. People around town also hired him to mow their lawns. It was a common sight to see him hugging the street curb with his riding mower, its little utility trailer loaded with gas can and weed trimmer. Mostly, I think folks thought they were doing Birdie a favor. He had a few customers who paid a going wage, but there were others who gave him a pittance, and not many thought to hand him a glass of cold water out the back door on a scorching mid-August day.

"I know that, Birdie, but there are other things to think about."

"Like what?"

"Well, you know, like groceries, meals, washing clothes, and getting to the doctor."

"I can eat at the café, Ivy May, or buy chicken to take home. They got good food at the café."

"You won't be lonesome, Birdie? I can't come down every week. It's too far." And then I added, "I've got my life, too, Birdie." My self-indulgent pity sounded pathetic, even to my biased ears.

"That's okay," he said.

I shrugged doubtfully. "Well, we can try it, I guess." And so we did. I found someone to come in once a week to wash clothes and clean and made arrangements at the bank for Birdie to draw out a certain amount of money each week for food. He could eat breakfast and lunch at the restaurant during the week, but he was on his own for suppers and weekends, so I stocked the refrigerator and stacked the freezer with microwavable meals.

* * *

Well, I thought as I pulled into the driveway, the early darkness of November not improving my mood, at least the weekend would provide an opportunity to see if things were working out for Birdie. The old house was lit up and pleasantly warm, the dining-room table—set with Mom's Sunday dishes no less—and two big Idaho bakers resting in the oven . . . but no Birdie. I went to the window and pulled apart the lace curtains my mother had so loved to look up the street. He was nowhere in sight. While I waited, I opened the mail lying on the cupboard and checked the freezer to find one half-eaten Dixie Cup. My microwave meals were evidently a big hit. A lonely Coke, some catsup, and a small jar of pickles were the only contents of the refrigerator. Then Birdie was at the back door, carrying a small box. "Where have you been?" I asked, giving him a hug. He seemed thin, but his usual talkative self.

"Oh, Willy Kotke died this afternoon. The hearse came and got him, but you couldn't see his face when they carried him out. He was all covered up. Do they always cover your face, Ivy May? I got a card and put a dollar in it and bought some donuts at the café to take over. Old Mrs. Kotke said thanks and it was nice of me to think of her and Willy."

"Oh, Birdie," I said, "you have such a big heart." Not for the first time, mine felt very small compared to his.

"I bet she'll be lonesome with Willy gone. I told her I'd shovel her sidewalk this winter. She said that'd be nice. I got chicken down at the café for supper, Ivy May. I told Ed to put in a little coleslaw, too." As we sat down to eat, I felt a sense of peace for the first time that day.

"Looks like the microwave dinners are working out," I said. "The freezer's empty. We'll have to go shopping tomorrow."

Birdie emptied the rest of the slaw on his plate and looked up. "Oh, I threw all that rotten stuff out, Ivy May. I didn't wanna get sick."

"But, Birdie, food will last several weeks in the freezer."

"It didn't smell good when I tried it, so I tossed it in the garbage. The whole works."

"But isn't the café closed after lunch? And what about Saturday and Sunday?"

"I get one of those sandwiches down at the station. They're wrapped in paper, so you can put 'em in the little microwave they got and heat 'em up."

"Birdie! Those are awful!"

"Wanna hear a joke, Ivy May? You know why they put that fancy fence up at the cemetery?"

"Nope," I said, fairly certain I would be hearing it again before the weekend was over. "Why?"

Birdie covered his mouth, giggled. "Cuz too many people are dyin' to get in."

"That's a good one, Birdie. You'll have to tell that one to Bill next time you see him."

"Bet he'll like it, Ivy May, won't he?"

"He'll love it," I answered, thinking it would serve Bill right to hear it more than just a few times.

Birdie was on a roll, clapping his hands together in excitement. "Last week when we was out to the cemetery throwin' away all the plastic flowers, Ed took a fake arm he found out at the landfill and stuck it right on top of a grave. It looked just like somebody was tryin' to get out of their coffin. Boy, Ivy May, people sure drove slow when they went by and saw that. It was real funny." I laughed along with Birdie, agreeing it was pretty humorous.

"Got any more stories, Birdie?"

Birdie thought for a minute. "You know why ladies never fart, Ivy May?" I shook my head. "Cuz they never stop talkin' long enough to build up any pressure."

It turned out to be a good weekend. We went grocery shopping. I told Birdie to pick out what he wanted. We came home with three packages of wieners, a loaf of Wonder bread, and a dozen cans of Festival corn. On Sunday we drove up to the truck stop in Worthington for dinner. Birdie said they had good chicken. I left for the long drive home in early afternoon with Birdie grinning and waving from the kitchen door. I shed tears off and on for the first thirty miles until I drove into Windom and stopped for gas. The convenience station had soft ice cream, and without thinking, I found myself buying a double-dipper.

* * *

The letter was postmarked Munger when it came in mid-December, but there was no return address, and I didn't recognize the writing on the front. My heart did an extra few thumps as I opened the envelope. Hopefully, it wasn't bad news, some well-meaning townsperson writing to let me know that Birdie wasn't staying in the lines. Instead, it was a Christmas card from a young woman who worked at the town office along with a folded newspaper article from the *Worthington Daily Globe* titled "Friend Sets Good Example for Others" by Kim McIntosh. I left my warmed-up morning coffee on the kitchen counter and sat down to read.

Each year, I look for a living example of the Christmas spirit—someone whose generosity inspires me to strive toward a more generous spirit of my own.

This time, I didn't have far to look. I knew from the day I met him that Birdie Ames had a soul that outshines most of those around him.

That day was my first in Munger, having just pulled in from a two-day move from Ohio. The 24-foot Ryder truck I had driven—with my three cats and one dog in the front seat next to me, and my car tagging along behind—sat in the front yard of the house I had just rented.

I unhooked the car and drove into the little town half a mile or so from my new home to see if I could find someone to help me unload. One by one, people shrugged. I was sure I was not the town's usual drop-in visitor. I next tried City Hall. Birdie was there and he quickly volunteered. He's no longer young and spry, and might not be able to carry larger pieces of furniture, he said, but he could surely handle boxes. The city clerk also rounded up a couple of city workers who could help on their lunch hour. I couldn't believe my good luck.

Two men sent over by my new place of employment helped the two Munger city workers on the larger and heavier pieces over their lunch hour. But Birdie. Birdie worked on and on, helping me carry in boxes and small tables and appliances. When we did finish, he didn't want pay, but I shoved my last $20 into his hand.

As I drove him back into town from my little acreage, I couldn't thank him enough. He smiled and said he may not be smart about some things, but he knows helping people is important in life. At one point, I even apologized for the dirt on my face after all our work. And he brought me up short by saying very matter-of-factly, "I don't care how you look. I just care how you act."

After that day, whenever he saw me, he would say, "There's my friend," to anyone within earshot. He would also offer to help with anything I might need, even if only to buy me a cup of coffee.

In the months since, I've watched him greet strangers with a smile and neighbors by name. I've watched him give someone his last $5 when asked. I've even watched him good naturedly take ribbing that went beyond affectionate to very obviously rude and insulting. I've watched, and I've learned.

"There's a good guy there," Birdie would say of someone who walked by. Or, "See that guy over there? I did some work for him. He said he couldn't pay me, but that's OK. I like to help." (There were a lot of those.) Even, "That guy just sounds mean. He doesn't really want to hurt me. He's a good guy." (And far too many of those.)

Birdie doesn't put anyone on a pedestal. And he may have a childlike view of the goodness in people, with a quickness to *forgive. But that just goes to show he obviously has it all over the rest of us who tend to treat others by a conscious or unconscious judgment of IQ.*

I don't know why Birdie says he isn't smart. I have asked, but he only shrugs and says that's what others have told him. I never bothered to find out what medical or mental condition might be involved. It doesn't seem that important. In fact, I've decided to tell him, the next time we talk, that he's not completely correct when he says he's not smart. And he shouldn't listen to anyone who tries to tell him that.

Truth is, he may not be smart about some things, or even in the ways some people would prefer him to be; but he's smart in the heart, and that beats smart in the head any day. When he says, "I just care how you act" and that he knows it's important to help people, Birdie Ames is clearly an example of the kind of generous spirit that we should all aspire to be all year long.

I folded the letter quietly, humbled that my brother, a simple man with a willing and loving heart, was a better neighbor, in the fullest sense of the word, than I could ever be.

* * *

No other Christmas greeting has quite measured up to that one.

Changing Places

With my head in the clouds, stuck in the sand, or very possibly some place much less lovely, I had always promised myself that I wouldn't let life just drift away, get lost in the mundane affairs of everyday living, but of course, I did just that . . . like most everybody else I know. And all too soon, confronted with middle age and then way beyond, I found myself desperately searching for the meaning of past years. I guess I was looking for that ego integrity that some know-it-all ideologue told us was necessary to attain in order to grow old with grace and peace.

I'm not exactly sure what ego integrity means, but I think it's something like coming to grips with who you are or aren't and being satisfied with whatever the hell that is. Bill found his whatever long before I even began looking for mine. He retired early and never looked back, content to smoke some cheap Carter Hall in his Dr. Grabow, putter in the wood shop, and count the boats on the lake, his thought on the whole affair simply being, "It is what it is, Iv." But it took a bit of doing for me to even contemplate that idyllic state of mind. For one thing, there was always the unfinished business of Birdie, and I bore the guilt of the same procrastination I had so faulted in my mother. I had always known Birdie's days in Munger were numbered. Then what? It was an inevitability that needed to be faced. Oh, I thought about it from time to time, but always with the excuse that decisions could wait until another, more opportune time . . . next summer, when the kids were out of college, after Maren's wedding, when Bill's prostate cancer was under control, or when I finally retired.

My wake-up jolt came out of the blue one Saturday when Bill and I were having afternoon coffee out on the deck. He tossed aside the monthly AARP magazine he'd been reading and asked, "What if you kick the bucket before Bird, Iv? Ever thought of that?" I scalded my throat on a big gulp of hot brew before I spit out, "You mean if I die first?"

"Could happen, you know," Bill said, shrugging. "No guarantee he's goin' first, is there?" Then he added, "You know, Iv, the next-door neighbors and your cousin Rusty and his wife, Betty, up the street are about the only folks in Munger who give a darn about Bird, and they're gettin' old. Anyway, let's face it; he's not their responsibility. I expect they've got their own golden years to deal with." Bill and I always laughed about that ridiculous name for the elder time of life, agreeing that about the only thing golden since the AARP card came in the mail was our pee. Bill reached for another oatmeal cookie and mused, "And to the young folks who've moved into town because of the cheap housing, he's just a funny old guy who's always lickin' a double-dipper and never stops grinnin'."

Barely containing my anger, I set my coffee down with enough force to slosh it onto the side table and shot back, "Well, it's not like I've been doing nothing these past seven years, Bill. Good God! I think I've honored my promise to Mom pretty well when it comes to Birdie. And it's not like he's been the only blip on my radar screen." I grabbed my mug and reached across to snatch Bill's, my peaceful afternoon shot to smithereens by the one question I didn't want to answer.

"Don't I even get to finish my coffee?" Bill asked, hanging on to his mug. "Don't get all riled up, Iv. I'm not saying you haven't done your part, but sometimes it's like you don't wanna hear the truth . . . even it bites you in the ass."

You'd better believe I found a bit of my ego integrity at that moment. I whirled and heaved my favorite mug over the deck railing as far as I could (without inflicting more damage to my cranky rotator cuff). It landed with a splash near the end of the dock, leaving Bill looking as surprised as all get-out. "Sweet Jesus!" he exclaimed, lifting his arm to shield his face, no doubt thinking the flower pot on the table was heading his way next. "Well, I'll say one thing for you, Iv," he laughed. "You've got one helluva arm!"

That afternoon must have been an omen of things to come. The next Tuesday evening, Helen Ann, one of Birdie's neighbors, called to apologetically share a few things she thought I ought to know. "I don't want to be a gossip, Ivy May, and you know I'm not, but there's talk goin' on uptown that Birdie's hangin' around with this

woman. Bob and I are kinda worried about him." Helen
Ann paused before continuing. "She's . . . well . . . got problems, too, like Birdie, but I think she knows more about
certain things than Birdie does, Ivy May . . . if you know
what I mean." There was an uncomfortable silence before
she added, "Bob says the guys up to the pool hall are . . .
well . . . talkin' pretty dirty to Birdie about it."

If the Millers were concerned enough to call, it had to
be something serious. Helen Ann and Bob were good folks,
the salt of the earth, my mother often said, who minded
their own business, but in a quiet way also looked out for
Birdie and often invited him over for a cup of coffee and a
piece of apple pie. Not many in Munger thought to do that.
I sensed that there was more to the story than Helen Ann
was comfortable in sharing, so I didn't pursue it—mostly,
though, because I didn't want to hear the details.

So instead I asked her about her garden and if she
were busy canning green beans, somehow always so much
tastier than the frozen ones. "Oh, sure, Ivy May, almost
thirty quarts already. They're Bob's favorite, you know."
Our conversation ended with Helen Ann's suggesting
I come down and check things out for myself. "Just to
make sure," she said, "that nothing bad happens to Birdie.
I know if your mother was here, she'd be real upset." That
was a colossal understatement. When I hung up the phone,
I turned to find Bill peeking in the doorway of the den
with a raised eyebrow and a smug told-you-so expression
on his face. By six o'clock the next morning I was headed
south to Munger.

* * *

The house was tidy, but it had a stale, musty smell, as if the windows hadn't been opened for a long time. Birdie wasn't there—uptown for morning coffee, I figured, so I headed for the café. I spotted him, alone in the back booth, dunking a donut in his coffee. As he looked up and motioned me back, I sensed something different about him: no grin, for one thing. "Hi, Bird," I said, sliding into the seat across from him. I reached over to cover his hand and asked, "What's up?" He was nervously swinging his head from side to side and constantly doing that irritating lip-smacking thing that drove me crazy. "What's wrong, Birdie? What's wrong? Are you taking your medicine?" My questions went unanswered. It was then I noticed the big abrasion on the top of his head. "What happened to your head, Birdie? Did you fall?"

"No. Don't think so. Just rubbed it a little, and the skin came off. Do you think I'd hit her, Ivy May? I don't think so, do you? She says if I hit her, she'll call the cops. Then what? What'll happen to me then?"

"Whoa, Birdie. Slow down. Who told you this?"

"Can't think of her name right now, but she lives over by the church. Think I should get married? She says we should get married and live in my house cuz it's bigger than hers. Think I'd hit her, Ivy May? Think I'd do it? I don't wanna go to jail. She says even if I hit her dog, she'll call the cops."

"Come on, Birdie, let's go home," I urged, handing his cap to him. "Let's get a double-dipper and go home."

"The guys at the Peanut Bar asked if she was goin' down on me, Ivy May. What's that mean?" The noisy morning coffee crowd in the café was suddenly quiet, all ears to our conversation in the back booth.

"Come on, Birdie," I said. "Let's go."

I asked for two double-dippers, a chocolate for Birdie and butter brickle for myself. The kid helping out at the bar shook the greasy hair out of his eyes, pulled his cap around so the bill faced backwards, and mumbled, "We don't got no cones. You want some in a dish?"

Birdie, standing behind me and smacking away the whole while, said, "That's okay, Ivy May. We can git one of those frozen Drumsticks down at the station."

※ ※ ※

Enjoying his Drumstick, Birdie trotted ahead of me as we headed toward his house. I was thinking the ice cream was a pitiful substitute for the double-dippers we got at Worthmore when we were kids. "Hey, Bird," I said, speeding up to walk beside him. "Remember the big cones we used to get? Boy, that was a lot of ice cream for a dime, wasn't it?"

"Think I'd hit her, Ivy May? Would they put me in jail?"

"Birdie, just forget about it. I'll tell you what. How about coming back with me for a few days? That would be fun, wouldn't it? Bill can take you fishing, and we can put pork chops on the grill."

Finally, Birdie grinned. "And git a double-dipper at that Dairy Queen we went to before, couldn't we, Ivy May?"

I put my arm around him and squeezed tight. "You better believe it, Bird. We can treat ourselves every day. First though, we'd better put something on that big sore on the top of your head. It looks awful."

* * *

Bad as it was, the whole affair proved to be the motivation I needed to make plans for Birdie's future . . . and, really, my own, too. I knew I had to get him out of Munger and some place close to Bill and me. I shared my dilemma with another teacher, and he asked if I had ever thought about an assisted-living arrangement for Birdie. It sounded like a great idea. Breaking the news to Birdie was hard, though. We both cried, especially when he said, "We can't just go and leave Marion out at the cemetery, Ivy May. He'll be all alone and sad."

"Oh, no, Birdie," I said. "Mom and Dad are there with him . . . and Grandpa Henry and Grandma Ada . . ."

"But it's not the same if I'm not there. Is it dark where Marion is? And what about my job? The guys'll be mad if I just up and quit, won't they? And how about my mower and wagon?" Birdie looked scared to death.

"You know what, kiddo? It's time to retire and enjoy life." What a bunch of baloney that was.

* * *

We had a yard sale, packed up Birdie's things, and sold the house. The folks in Munger had a little going-away party for Birdie, even collected a few bucks to send him off.

142

Helen and Bob seemed relieved. I couldn't blame them. I knew they had been shouldering a good bit of what was really my responsibility. "You're doin' the right thing, Ivy May," Helen Ann said as she helped me wipe out the refrigerator. "Birdie needs to be with family." Then she added, "Your mother would be real happy."

Labels

For "seniors"—a silly tag I love to hate and just a tiresome euphemism for what we're usually thought of, namely old poops—there's a whole lot more to life than blissful winters in Arizona chatting with the snowbirds next door about the importance of fiber in one's diet, time shares, or how to maximize those senior discounts, like getting three cents off a gallon of gas, providing the purchase is at least twenty dollars.

Ah, yes, behind the façade of carefree retirement there lurks the impending possibility and probability of such mysterious and potentially dreadful things as elderly waivers, case mixes, spend-downs, and just understanding how the "system" works . . . or doesn't. I'm thinking I'll be somewhat prepared to stay afloat, or maybe, with a little luck, even navigate the treacherous rapids when the time comes, all because of Birdie. Admittedly, the complexity of this chapter of my life will confront me when things aren't working upstairs nearly as well as they did a few years back.

Birdie, though obviously disabled and pushing sixty-five, was in trouble. He simply wasn't in the system. Ruthie and Job Ames had been strong conservatives who valued independence and personal responsibility. They hadn't had much time for folks who sat around expecting a handout. They wouldn't have dreamed of shirking their responsibilities. My brother was their son, flesh of their flesh. That was admirable and worked . . . until they were gone. Then he needed to be in the system to survive, and that required a diagnosis. Somewhere in that process, the friendly, caring man called Birdie disappeared and became Birdsel Ames, a mentally retarded, bipolar, obsessive-compulsive adult with "behaviors" and a little dementia. And yes, lest I forget the lip-smacking, even that had a label: dyskinesia.

Oddly, most who knew him acknowledged that he was slow when it came to the three Rs, but plenty smart about operating machinery and reading people and, to their chagrin, often blunt in his assessment of them. One psychologist said it was a filter problem; another one determined Birdie was disinhibited. I never accepted the bipolar diagnosis, a disorder I always thought involved giant mood swings. Birdie only had one mood, happy, but even that incredibly positive trait had a downside away from Munger. In his new world, it meant he was manic, because no one in his right mind could possibly be as happy as he was.

My mother's ancient lawyer gave me a sound bit of advice. "If you expect to help your brother, Ivy May, your best bet is to go to court and be appointed his guardian. Otherwise, nobody will talk to you about a darn thing." The old codger, who sported the most generous growth of nose hair I had ever seen, was right. Nobody would, but armed with a notarized piece of paper to that effect, I found the system opened up, at least a small crack.

In order to claim Birdie as my father's dependent child and thereby eligible for social-security benefits, I had to establish his disability. My mother's family doctor helped me jump that hurdle when he signed an affidavit that Birdie was not able to conduct his own affairs, but the regional Social Security representative was not so easily convinced when I finally got her on the phone. "The problem, Mrs. Hansen," she said, "is that we don't know when Mr. Birdsel Ames became retarded." She raised her voice and began to speak very slowly, as if that would help me understand a very involved situation which was obviously too profound for an old fool like me. "We would need to know the date of onset of Mr. Ames's disability in order to determine his eligibility to legally draw on his father's Social Security. Without significant proof, I'm afraid . . ." Her voice drifted off, and I could sense the conversation was coming to an end.

I suppose I sort of lost it then when I raised my voice and enunciated slowly, "Well, I'm pretty sure he didn't just wake up one morning and find he'd lost his brains."

Dear old Bill just happened to be in the kitchen, waiting for Mr. Coffee to stop gurgling, when I slammed the receiver down. "Not goin' so good, huh?" he ventured, poised to make a dash for his den if the situation should warrant it.

"You know what, Bill?" I said. "Maybe I should just drive Birdie over to St. Cloud and let the old bag talk to him for five minutes. I bet she'd get the picture mighty quick. Good God, I hate this bureaucratic crap!"

"Well, I suppose they've got to be careful, Iv. You know how they're always talkin' about the fraud in the system."

"Thanks for your profound input, Bill. You're such a help."

Within a month, my brother had been to the mental health clinic three times. He needed a diagnosis. The first session, the psychiatrist gave Birdie five numbers to remember and said he'd be asking him to repeat them, in backward order, in about fifteen minutes. Birdie just grinned, but I was thinking that if inability to do that task signaled dementia, most of the folks I knew, Bill and I included, were in deep doo. A few similar tests were enough for the good doctor to write the word "dementia" at the bottom of his chart. When I explained the need to establish Birdie's disability from birth, he suggested an MRI of his brain and, for good measure, maybe some psychological testing to determine his IQ. Good Lord, I thought, it sounded like we were talking about an IEP to get Birdie into an elementary school special-ed program instead of trying to get a sixty-four-year-old man some assistance.

By this time, I was on a mission. Being a teacher, I thought it might be possible to find some old school records in Munger that would support my claim of Birdie's disability. No such luck. It seemed nobody saw the need a half century ago to label a slow student. A few Us on a report card were about the extent of it. There was nothing in his medical history either, just notations about a bout with whooping cough sixty years before, some hernia repair in later life, and the usual assorted minor injuries and illnesses. And there was no possibility of getting the old timers in Munger to sign their names as witnesses of Birdie's disability. They were all resting in the cemetery south of town.

Thankfully, I had never been an efficient housekeeper. The upper shelves of our bedroom closets were stacked with shoe boxes, nary a one holding a pair of shoes but rather decades of canceled checks, business letters, and old Christmas cards. Bill asked me more than once why I was bent on filling all those boxes with stuff I'd never need. "I just haven't had time to sort through things," I answered.

"Oh, yeah? And when's that gonna happen?" was his response. Well, it did happen on a rainy day in late September, when I decided to tackle the upstairs bedroom closet. I started with a large shoe box marked "1991-Mom's papers." Gone eighteen years already, I thought as I blew off the dust and dumped the contents on the bed . . . her driver's license, marriage certificate, my father's death certificate, some papers held together by a doubled rubber band, and of all things, Birdie's birth certificate, and on the third line, written in Dr. Paget's nearly illegible hand, the words "severely asphyxiated." Viola! Birdie was in! My jubilation balloon lost air, however, when the social worker told me it really didn't matter since he'd be on an elderly waiver in a couple of months anyway.

* * *

For the next seven years, things sort of worked. Birdie liked his assisted living arrangement. There were things to do, places to go, and he scribbled his name down for every outing. He walked downtown most days the weather was decent and stopped for a drumstick or an egg roll from the deli at Coborn's Grocery. Sunday was set aside for dinner at our house—fried chicken, if possible, lots of vegetables, and pie or a double-dipper for dessert. But there were some bumps in the road, too, like a local hair salon's apologetic complaint that Birdie's stopping in for free coffee every morning was getting to be a bit of a nuisance. When they asked him to leave, he laughed and said, "I'm in no hurry." The psychologist said Birdie wasn't picking up on social cues.

About that same time, Birdie became obsessed with haircuts, the shorter and more often the better. Bill's barber said he didn't quite know what to do. Birdie was in his shop every day wanting his head shaved. He was uncomfortable with taking Birdie's money, but didn't know how to go about saying no to "the poor old fellow" without hurting his feelings. And then there was the afternoon police search for him when rode off on his bicycle one morning and didn't return for lunch. I was frantic when I got the call he was missing. Birdie wouldn't be able to explain where he lived if he were lost. "Oh, calm down, Iv," Bill said. "He's probably just sittin' down at J's havin' a piece of pie." And that's where we found him.

I persuaded myself that these little incidents weren't a big deal, and they weren't really. Bill reminded me I did a few goofy things, too, like backing out of the garage and smack into the charcoal grill. The grill survived, but it was a little hard on the rear bumper and the rotisserie chicken. And another time, when I was backing out the car to take Birdie home, I didn't heed his warning. "Be careful, Ivy May. You're gettin' too close to the wall." I managed to take part of the garage frame with me and left the right side rearview mirror dangling on the end of a mass of wires. "Oh, shit!" I said. "Look what I did."

Birdie covered his mouth and started to giggle. "Should I go tell Bill you didn't mean to do it, Ivy May? He won't be mad if I say you didn't mean to."

* * *

Then, overnight, the bumps in the road became potholes. Birdie fell and broke his hip, and for some unknown reason, he was suddenly incontinent. Walkers and Depends became the order of the day, and assisted living was no longer a good fit for Birdie's mental and physical needs.

See You Next Sunday

I can't complain that no one thought to forewarn me of time's fast-forward mode. For goodness' sake, poets have been versifying about it forever. Wasn't it the Bard of Avon who personified it as "Devouring Time" and went on to lament, "Like as the waves make towards the pebbled shore, so do our minutes hasten to their end"? My own mother started drilling it into my head before I started first grade at Shady Nook and never let up until I left for college. "Do something useful," she was fond of saying. "You're not going to be around forever, you know."

When I was thirteen and Mom caught me reading some dog-eared *True Romance* magazines I'd borrowed from Dorie Ann and tucked under my mattress to pore over during my weekly upstairs cleaning chores, she burned them in the cookstove and scolded, "Lost time is never found, Ivy May. Don't be wasting your time on trash." And even in the final days of her long life, she pressed on, "Ivy May, don't be letting your life drift away. You'll wake up one morning like I did, realize the end isn't far off, and spend your last days frantically wondering just what happened to all those years. You can't get them back, Ivy May. They're gone." Ah, yes, fast-forward, indeed, and no rewind.

But mostly we don't do what we know we should, our rationalization being there's always tomorrow, that today is just sort of a dress rehearsal for the command performance far down the road. But suddenly I was there, and I knew it for sure one fall morning when I ran into a former school colleague at the post office. "Joanne, it's so good to see you," I said, giving her a friendly hug. Then I remembered that Bill and I hadn't made it to her fiftieth birthday party earlier in the summer. I apologized, saying we had been out of town, probably visiting the kids.

Joanne started laughing. "Oh my God, Iv, that was four years ago. You're losing it!" There it was . . . the ugly truth. Somehow, four years of my life had slipped away, unaccounted for.

Then it seemed there was a thundering avalanche of reminders that Iv Hansen, aka Ivy May Ames, had become what she most dreaded, an old lady. Dr. Simon, my cardiologist, suggested a pacemaker might put a little more spring in my step. It did. When relatives visited, we talked mostly about our numerous ailments, encounters of the medical kind, and such scintillating topics as cremation and the cost and availability of cemetery plots. Adding insult to injury, my six-year-old grandson asked me during a visit if he could have my antique coffee grinder when I died. "I don't plan on leaving just quite yet," I told him.

"No," he said, "but you will, Grandma. Then can I have it? You could tape my name on the bottom so nobody else gets it." Good God, I thought, if a first-grader can see the writing on the wall, where is my head? I surmised there were others, as well, wondering about what was going to happen to my meager worldly treasures when I was gone. And there were little things, too, like my strange attempt to make a phone call on the TV remote and giving my hair a good mist of air freshener instead of hair spray one morning, which contributed to my realization that not only had time slipped away, but also possibly my mind. Perhaps, mostly sadly, I lived in a foreign land of regret, unattained goals, and dreams . . . things of another life, and, ironically, not caring about what I used to care about, but caring that I didn't care.

Birdie was a part of my senior God moment, too. During the yearly care-plan review, his case manager pushed a sizable packet entitled "Making Informed Life and Death Health Care Decisions" across the table, cleared her throat, and advised that an excellent goal for the coming year would be the development of a health-care directive for Birdie. "Talk to Birdsel about what kind of care he wants at the end of his life, Iv." She shoved her glasses up on her nose and added, "I'm sure you've already completed one for yourself. It's so important that our children don't have to deal with this issue."

I wanted to tell her I hadn't really been thinking a lot about how to spare my children from the traumatic experience of my last days on Earth. After a half century of being there for them, I felt entitled to any little disruption I might cause in their lives. Some hair pulling, gnashing of the teeth, and keening at the wailing wall would not be an excessive show of grief, at least not from my point of view.

Then Delores went on to offer some suggestions to guide my thinking down a desired path. For the life of me, I couldn't see myself discussing any of them with Birdie. What would I say? "Birdie, do you want one glass or two glasses of water when you get to the end?" or "How much morphine do you think you'll want before you meet your Maker face to face?" or "If you get a bad cold, do you want to just cough through it or would you like a teaspoon of Robitussin?" Egad! Birdie would be scared witless. He would have both sides of his cheeks rubbed off before nightfall and a couple of toenails uprooted as well.

And it didn't take much to set Birdie off. His self-abuse was a serious problem. Over the years it had escalated so alarmingly that his personal safety became a critical factor in his care. He was especially obsessed with rubbing his face and arms until blood flowed or deep purple bruises appeared, and he'd use any instrument handy to pry off his finger- and toenails. "The poor old guy's just bored out of his gourd," was Bill's take on the matter. "What's he supposed to do all day, Iv . . . color a picture or two and pretend he can read the morning paper?" I assured Birdie's case manager he'd always enjoyed inflicting a little physical pain on himself, that the present state of affairs, while problematic, was not all that strange. That seemed to somewhat allay their fears of liability, but they still suggested Birdie see a behavior therapist. She only lasted one session, her complaint being Birdie asked her what kind of lawn mower she had, if her husband mulched their lawn, and why she wore her glasses on the top of her head.

"I'm the one who's in charge of asking the questions, Birdsell," she reminded him. Birdie just grinned and told her about the John Deere riding mower he used to drive when he worked for the city. I guess the therapist wasn't much interested, because she pushed Birdie's thick three-ring binder of patient history across the table and said, "I don't believe Mr. Ames is a good candidate for behavior therapy. Drug therapy would probably be a more viable option."

Drug therapy was a slippery slope, with Birdie sliding quickly to the bottom. It was a trial-and-error attempt to treat multiple disorders, plus seventy years of mostly negative social experiences. Even schoolyard bullies sometimes end up in assisted living and long-term care and continue their despicable treatment of fellow residents they deem less worthy than themselves. "Stay away from me, you dumb ass!" one cross resident hollered at Birdie, lifting his cane to strike.

Birdie cried at first, but then grinned and said, "It's okay. He probably don't know any better." That had always been Birdie's take on that sort of thing. It was the bully who owned the problem of rudeness and ignorance. "Sticks and stones . . ." he'd say, shrugging his shoulders . . . but I could see the hurt in his eyes.

* * *

In the end, I didn't have to worry about Birdie's last days. He went gently into that good night, as the poet says, hopefully comfortably hydrated and without pain.

It didn't seem right, though, the quiet departure. Life is such a wondrous, complicated affair, so fraught with every emotion humanly possible, that trumpets should blare, bells peal, comets streak across the sky, and loud alleluias ring out, especially for a life well lived. At least in Munger, the Presbyterian steeple bell would have tolled Birdie's seventy-nine years and set the folks to wondering who had passed on. But there was only a predawn phone call on a windy March morning and a brief but gentle message from the wellness nurse. "Iv, Birdie was unresponsive this morning." And then a quiet moment before she added, "We called Olson's as you had directed, but we'll wait for you to come."

Our last words had been simple ones. "Thanks for the good dinner," Birdie said as I entered the security code to admit us. Then he added, as always, "See you next Sunday."

"Love you, Bird," I answered.

"Love you, too, Ivy May."

* * *

"Oh, Birdie," I whispered to the bag next to me, "I hope Marion met you at the golden gates and it's bright as day there." Suddenly, I braked, made a sharp right, and, without signaling, headed east on Ninth Street to the Dairy Queen. "Birdie," I said, "I'm thinking a big chocolate double-dipper would taste pretty darn good right now. And you know what? Let's just spill all we want. Let 'er rip, kiddo!"

SEE YOU NEXT SUNDAY

The driver behind me, who obviously didn't know squat about keeping a safe distance between himself and the car in front, especially if the driver were a white-haired old lady, honked his horn to let me know he wasn't thinking kind thoughts of me. "Oh, shove it!" I muttered. I swear that the Macy's bag jumped a little, and I could see Birdie grin from ear to ear.